D0533472

UAT

Please renew or return items by the date shown on your receipt

www.hertsdirect.org/libraries

Renewals and enquiries: 0300 123 4049

Textphone for hearing or speech impaired 0300 123 4041

Hertfordshire

H46 644 015 5

ATTACK OF THE BALLISTIC BLANKET

SAM HAY

Catnip

For Alice and Archie

CATNIP BOOKS
Published by Catnip Publishing Ltd
14 Greville Street
London EC1N 8SB

First published 2013
1 3 5 7 9 10 8 6 4 2

Text © 2013 Sam Hay
Illustrations © 2013 Tom Morgan-Jones

A CIP catalogue record for this book is available from the British Library

ISBN 978-1-84647-164-3

Printed in Poland

www.catnippublishing.co.uk

CHAPTER 1

Sprockets! Blooming sprockets! Six of the blighters had scuppered my Saturday and to be perfectly frank I was pretty cheesed off about it.

I was meant to be cycling up to Mulligan's pond to build a raft with my best mate, Mark. But then the sprockets went on my bike, and our plans were pancaked.

What are sprockets anyway? They sound like some sort of nasty vegetable you'd try and hide under your knife. Or a foot fungus you'd be embarrassed to show your mates. I think my dad just dreamed them up to prevent me from going to the pond. Secretly, I think he just wanted me to stay and help out in his shop (again).

That's what I do on Saturday mornings, and usually

I don't mind. After all, the pay is okay and it's not hard work – there are no customers and mostly I just sit around with my feet up reading magazines (munching a doughnut or two from the bakery next door, if I'm lucky). But today was supposed to be different. Me and Mark had plans . . .

'Don't worry, son,' said Dad, sticking his head out the back. 'I'll get you going in no time. I've just got a bit of paperwork to finish first.'

My heart sank. 'A bit of paperwork' to Dad meant sitting in his office for hours searching for invoices. I looked at my bike and sighed. It wasn't fair. Dad could fix it in an instant, with his eyes shut and a super-size strawberry doughnut in each hand. That's what he does, you see. He's a repair man.

Jimmy Kirk,
he'll make
it work!

says the sign outside the shop. And it's true. When it comes to white goods, Dad's a miracle man. If your cooker's kaput, or your dishwasher's dead, give him a call, because he can get any old bit of tat up and running.

Which explains why our house is full of junk. Though some of it *is* quite cool. How many people do you know with a full-size juke box in their bedroom? I've got one and it's bigger than me. It doesn't play anything you'll have heard of, but it's got fantastic flashing lights. We've also got a chocolate fountain in the bathroom (Dad likes to snack while he soaks), six cuckoo clocks in the hall (the ticking helps Mum sleep) and a telly the size of a hippo in the lounge, which is not so cool. The thing is horrible. Truly embarrassing. The sumo wrestler of the surround-sound world.

Dad's shop's just same. It's like an electrical graveyard full of disembowelled hair dryers, headless hoovers and two-ton tellies that no one wants. Some of it works. Most of it doesn't. 'Work in progress,' Dad calls it.

Sometimes I wonder how he makes any money. He says his customers come when I'm at school. They certainly don't bother us on Saturdays (and to be honest, I'm quite glad).

You're probably wondering why Dad needs my help. Well he doesn't, not really. But for some reason he reckons working is good for kids. (If I'd been born a hundred years ago I'd probably have spent my Saturdays stuck up someone's chimney!) Plus Dad's hopeless at paperwork and Saturday is the day he locks himself in his office and tries to make sense of all the scraps of paper he's got stuffed in his accounts book.

Anyway, there I was that Saturday, stranded in Dad's shop with a dead bike at my feet and nothing else to do except start on the doughnuts (Dad had bought a box to cheer me up), when something really weird happened. A doughnut nearly killed me. Really, it did.

You see, just as I was tucking in, a customer appeared in the shop. Honestly, one minute it was just me and the doughnuts, the next there she was, bold as brass. I was so shocked I gulped in a mouthful of air when I should have been swallowing and a lump of sugary gunge got wedged in my windpipe.

For a second I thought I'd die. Death by doughnut! I clutched my throat and gagged, and then I gagged some more. I think I probably turned purple, or blue, or pink maybe. Because the woman who'd arrived in the shop obviously spotted I was suffocating to death. She glared at me crossly for a moment, as if deciding whether to save me. Then she stalked over and gave me a hefty thump between the shoulder blades.

If the doughnut didn't kill me, I was pretty sure she was about to. Boy did it hurt. I felt my teeth rattle in my skull. I'm not sure whether it was from fear that she might do it again, or whether it was the shock of seeing a customer in Dad's shop. But somehow the tiny piece of cake that was blocking my breathing tubes suddenly dislodged itself and thankfully I found I could taste air again.

CHAPTER 2

I gawped. This lady might have just saved my life, but she was also the freakiest looking critter I'd ever laid eyes on. She was a monster. Truly! For starters, she towered over me. That's not hard. Most people do. I'm short for my age. (I'm not officially panicking yet; Dad says he didn't sprout until he was 15, and I'm only 12, so there's still hope.) But it wasn't just her height that dwarfed me; she was as broad as she was tall. Her hair was red. Her face was, too. And she had the biggest hands I'd ever seen. Like massive shovels. But it was her eyes that were the scariest bit – they were black and purple with huge dark circles round them. She looked like she hadn't slept for a century or two.

For a few seconds I just stared. Then from somewhere in the pit of my belly I managed to winkle up a shred of professionalism. After all, she was a potential customer. *My* customer. My *first ever* customer. And somehow I managed to spring into action.

You see, I'd rehearsed this bit, like a fire drill I suppose. In the eventuality of a real customer setting foot in the shop, this is what I had to do:

1. Hide doughnut box.
2. Wipe sticky fingers discreetly on jeans.
3. Stand up and greet customer warmly.
4. Get Dad.

That was it. My four-point plan.

But I was so shaken up by the whole death-by-doughnut experience that I jumped straight to point three of my plan, which was a shame because it meant the doughnut box landed on the floor, and the hand that I held out to her was a sweaty palm full of strawberry jam.

'Thank you . . .' I croaked '. . . for er, um . . . saving me . . .' (And very nearly beating me to death!) I swallowed and then winced. I now had a super-sore throat to go along with the pain between my shoulder blades where she'd thumped me. 'Welcome to Kirk's Repairs,' I finally managed to squeak.

She ignored my jam hand (wisely) and peered around the shop. 'Where's Jimmy?' she growled.

I gulped. Her voice sounded like an old bloke's. An old bloke who smoked a pipe . . . *six* pipes (all at the same time).

I stuttered and stumbled, and tried to explain that he was out back. But she held up a big hand to silence me. Then she opened her coat and produced a black nylon bag. 'This needs mending,' she said, throwing it at me.

It looked like a rolled-up sleeping bag. I wasn't sure what to do next. I mean Dad could fix anything, of course he could. But a *sleeping bag*? What could possibly be wrong with it?

I was about to explain that we didn't do sewing jobs, not even for extremely intimidating women who saved the life of small shop assistants. But then she bent down, wiggled one thick podgy finger and beckoned me closer. Reluctantly I edged forward, still holding her bag. Then she fixed one beady eye on me (the other eyeball suddenly veered off to the side, as though keeping a look-out in case anyone came in).

'Listen,' she growled, peering into my face.

I tried hard to concentrate, but I couldn't stop staring at her roving eye – the one that was currently doing a fandango around her face.

She pointed at the sleeping bag. 'That thing won't do as it's told,' she growled. 'It's got a mind of its own, see. And I don't like that. Fix it!'

I smiled. And gulped. A sleeping bag that wouldn't

do what it was told? Er . . . right! Clearly she was mad. Barking mad. Positively baying-at-the-moon mad. But I was too scared to say anything other than: 'Of course . . .'

She frowned. Then straightened up. 'Tell Jimmy Gloria will be back at dawn. Here . . .' she raked around in one of her coat pockets and produced a small purple purse. 'Half now, half later, just as Jimmy likes it.'

Instinctively I held out my hand to take the money. Then she turned and was gone. For someone so large she moved like a whippet. Actually she didn't completely go. A faint, stinky smell of sweat and pipe smoke lingered in the shop long after she'd gone. I wrinkled my nose. I didn't like it. I definitely didn't like it.

CHAPTER 3

The purse felt strangely heavy in my hand, and I was tempted to peek inside. You see, I was pretty sure this wasn't the normal way people would pay for a repair job. A 'mafia hit-man' sort of job, maybe, but a 'Jimmy Kirk, he'll make it work' sort of job, no! Absolutely not!

Mind you, I'll admit I didn't have much experience to go on. But I was pretty sure this wasn't how it worked. And anyway, since when did my dad repair sleeping bags?

Then I had an idea. Maybe there was another shop at the other end of the high street that *did* mend sleeping bags. And she'd just got confused. But I looked around Dad's shop, stuffed full of washing machines and microwaves and long-dead deep-fat fryers. One glance would have told her she was in the wrong place. No, as I'd thought before, she was bonkers. Pure and simple, mad as cheese.

Crazy people scare me. They're just so unpredictable! I definitely didn't want to be here at dawn when she came back to collect her bag and realised her mistake. I shuddered at the thought. Then I peeped into the purse and nearly had a heart attack! It was stuffed full of gold coins. Dozens of them. For a millisecond I thought they might actually be real, but then I rolled my eyes and laughed out loud. They were obviously chocolate. Mrs Crazy Eyes probably did all her shopping with chocolate coins. No one was going to argue with her, were they?

I picked up one of the coins and held it up to the light, looking for the edge of the foil to pick it off. But I couldn't see it. And then I did a very weird thing. I've no idea why – shopkeeper's instinct maybe – but I put the coin in my mouth and bit it. Big mistake! I nearly broke my tooth!

'Aaargh!' I yelped. It certainly wasn't chocolate.

Then I stood there, weighing up the weirdness of it all. I mean, why would a scary woman (quite possibly, the scariest woman in the world) have come into our shop to tell me her sleeping bag was misbehaving and then leg it, leaving a handful of gold coins for me to sort it out?

Looking back, it was at this point that I should have fetched Dad. After all, there was nothing in my Saturday-shop-assistant book of rules that covered any of this. But unfortunately I didn't.

Instead, I bent down and cautiously opened the bag. I'm not sure what I was expecting to find, but a flood of relief instantly coursed through my bones, because something big and heavy and very familiar fell out . . . a plug!

I grinned. It wasn't a sleeping bag after all. It was something that *did* actually belong in our shop – an electric blanket. Mrs Crazy Eyes wasn't as mad as I'd imagined. (Mind you, it still didn't explain the gold coins.)

I hauled the thing out and unfolded it on the floor. I'm not sure why, but I suddenly felt the urge to lie down on the thing and see how it felt. So I did. That was my second mistake! Because as I stretched out like a star and got all nice and comfy, I heard a clunk, then a clank, followed by another clunk and then a gentle whirring sound starting up underneath me and the blanket began to shudder slightly. I tried to sit up, but the vibrating got worse, and I couldn't quite do it. I just sort of floundered like a bug on its back. Then there was a sudden blast of air from underneath the blanket, and the front door of the shop crashed open.

At this point, I really should have started screaming, because this definitely wasn't normal behaviour for an electric blanket, certainly one that wasn't even plugged in! But I didn't. I was too freaked out to do anything. And then it was too late, because both sides of the blanket flipped up and over, smothering me in the middle.

'Hey!' I yelped, finally finding my voice. But my cries were muffled against the sides of the blanket. I thrashed about wildly, but it made no difference, I was now the human filling in a blanket omelette.

I could barely breathe. I pounded my arms, fighting to get free, but I was held fast. Then I began to panic. This was it. I was about to be suffocated by an electric blanket . . .

But there was more to come – the blooming thing started to rise! I stopped thrashing and lay there stunned. We were definitely moving off the ground. Then after a few seconds the blanket stopped rising and hovered in the air until with a sudden rush of energy it hurtled forward and shot out of the shop door.

CHAPTER 4

Okay, okay, I know what you're thinking. What a load of baloney. That's what I'd be thinking too, if it wasn't for the fact that at that moment I was rocketing up into the air in a rolled-up electric blanket!

After a few minutes it stopped climbing, levelled out a bit, and then slowly the blanket began to unfold. That's when I very nearly fell off. The wind was so strong it blasted me over to the side and I had to scrabble around for something to cling on to. Of course there wasn't anything, because electric blankets don't have handles.

'Help!' I shouted, gripping the edge with my fingertips. 'Up here!' I yelled, hopefully. Then I remembered it was Saturday. And everyone was probably far too busy shopping to notice me.

'HEEELP!' I tried again. The wind was ripping at my fingers. Any second now I'd loose my grip and I'd be splattered on the high street below.

'Press the air-shield lever or you'll be a gonner!' shrieked a small voice I couldn't see.

'What?'

'The air-shield lever! It's under the ejector booster. But for pity's sake don't touch the destruct spinet, or we'll both be toast!'

What? Who was shouting at me? And what on *earth* was it on about?

'Quick, man!' yelled the voice. 'PRESS THE BUTTON!'

'But there *are* no buttons,' I wailed. 'It's an electric blanket!"

'Look under the ignition switch, where you turned the rotten thing on.'

'But I didn't turn it on. I just lay down on it.'

'Well do it again, then.'

So I did. Somehow I managed to roll on to my back and spread myself out like a starfish, my hands wrapped round the edges of the blanket, my eyes staring up at the clouds that were whizzing past.

'Wiggle your head a bit more!'

And as I did, I heard a CLUNK! and a ZIP! and instantly the wind disappeared, as though an invisible bubble had suddenly surrounded me. I sat up cautiously, expecting at any moment to be blown away to my doom. But all I did was bump my head, presumably on the invisible air-shield thingy!

I looked around. To the left was a flock of gulls, surfing the thermals, completely oblivious to me. To the right a distant aeroplane disappeared into the clouds. And that was it. Nothing else apart from clouds. I inched across to one side and peered down. 'Aaargh!' I gasped. The town below had vanished and was now replaced with fields and sheep and the occasional leafless tree, all hurtling past in a blur . . .

'Careful,' called the voice. 'You're sitting right above the trap door!'

I jerked back into the centre of the blanket and it wobbled violently.

'Watch out! You'll sink us both!'

'Who are you?' I yelled. 'And . . . er . . . *where* are you?'

The voice didn't reply. But then I saw something

green appearing through the left-hand corner of the blanket. And a strange reptilian face emerged, followed by the rest of it. As it pulled out its tail, it sat shyly in the corner, boggling me.

'You're a lizard,' I said stupidly.

'A chameleon actually, an Antarctic chameleon. My name is Brimstone . . . And you are . . .' It glanced at my chest. 'Thomas Kirk from Kirk's Repairs.'

I looked down. I'd forgotten the name badge, which I wore whenever I worked in Dad's shop. Then I looked back at the chameleon. 'I didn't know lizards could talk,' I said stupidly.

The creature fixed me with a sarcastic stare. 'And I didn't know small boys could fly electric blankets . . . except they can't, can they!' it added pointedly.

I didn't like the 'small boy' thing, especially as the creature was no bigger than a bread roll. And it wasn't exactly a looker either, with its sludge-green skin, cone-shaped head and bug eyes. But it was kind of cool too. 'So . . . er . . . can you change colour?' I said, trying to make conversation. Years ago I'd borrowed a library book about reptiles and it was the only fact about chameleons I could remember.

But before it could answer, the blanket suddenly jolted sideways, tossing us both in the air. I cracked my head on the air-shield thingy before thudding back down.

'How do we stop this thing?' I yelped.

'You can't,' said the chameleon. 'It's a Snooze Cruiser . . .'

'A what?'

'A Snooze Cruiser – a vintage model – made by Macdonald and Aziz . . .'

'Who?'

'Macdonald and Aziz, the flying carpet manufacturers. Of course, this model is frightfully rare now,' the creature went on. 'Very much from the golden age of travel – only thirty were ever made.'

I glanced down at the blanket. It didn't look special. It was pink and faded and slightly mouldy at the edges. And in the middle was a horrible stain, as though someone had piddled on it.

'But it's a touch unreliable,' sighed the chameleon.

The blanket suddenly jerked upwards, throwing us both into the air once more.

'Oi!' I yelped, as I banged my head for the second time.

'It doesn't like to be talked about,' whispered the creature. 'Perhaps we'd better change the subject.'

'Fine, but how can we make it land?'

'There's an instruction manual inside one of the pockets . . .'

'But there *are* no pockets!' I protested.

The chameleon blinked at me, then cocked his head

to one side. 'The trouble with humans is most of them never learn how to see things properly.'

'But there's nothing to see,' I said stubbornly.

Brimstone shrugged. 'It doesn't matter. Even if you *could* find the instructions, Snooze Cruisers tend to do their own thing . . . and anyway, stopping the blanket is the least of your problems, because you've stolen a witch's blanket!'

'I didn't steal it!'

'Not only have you stolen a witch's blanket,' the chameleon went on. 'But you've stolen a *stolen* witch's blanket! The woman who brought it to the shop was Gloria Bladderwart, a grim stench witch of the lowest order. But the blanket didn't belong to her. She stole it from someone else. Someone much scarier! Trust me, you're sunk. You might as well head out the escape hatch without a para-cape . . .'

'Look, I've no idea what a para-cape is,' I said feeling slightly cross now. 'But I didn't steal the blanket. I just got tangled up in it, by mistake.'

'Won't wash, excuses never do.'

'But it's the truth!'

'Oh, the truth is never to be trusted,' said Brimstone,

'and totally useless when dealing with witches. They hate the truth. If I were you I'd come up with a big fat fib, and fast, because you've triggered the blanket's homing device, which means very soon we'll be arriving at the Lighthouse of Souls.'

'A lighthouse?'

'Yes, but not one of those nice save-ships-at-sea types. The Lighthouse of Souls is home to a truly ghastly witch by the name of Pallidia Black. And meeting her means certain death for us both, probably. Trust me, jumping would be better.'

'Ha!' I scoffed. 'Don't be ridiculous! I'll just explain to this lighthouse keeper, Pallidia whatever her name is, that it's all been a dreadful mistake . . .'

'A word of advice,' Brimstone interrupted. 'Whatever she says, don't look at her eyes!'

'What?'

'I wish I could help more, but I can't,' Brimstone said turning away. 'It's just too dangerous.' Then he disappeared back into the invisible hole he had climbed out of.

'Wait!' I yelled. 'Come back!' But the chameleon had gone.

I shivered. Dark clouds were drifting over the sun, and the sky had turned a steely grey. As I glanced below, I could see we were running out of land, too. A jagged coastline was approaching, and beyond that, the sea – huge, dark and menacing – and standing on the horizon, a tiny white spec in the distance, was a lighthouse.

Panic swept over me. Of course I didn't really believe in witches, but until today I hadn't believed in flying blankets, either. I searched desperately for a control panel, or a pocket containing the instructions on how to land the thing. But there was nothing. No buttons, no dials. Just blanket. And the lighthouse was growing ever closer. I stopped looking then and studied it instead.

Tall and forbidding, it stood a mile or so off the coast amidst a half-submerged rocky reef. Much of its white paint had been battered away by the sea and several windows were bricked up. At the top was a glass dome where the light must be. I craned to see if it was switched on – it wasn't – but as we got closer it suddenly burst into life, trapping me in its beam like a moth.

My eyes felt like they were burning in its brightness.

I tried to shield them with my hands, but the blanket lurched violently forward, hurtling faster as though it was being sucked into quicksand. Any second I expected to be splattered into the side of the lighthouse or dashed to bits on the rocks below. I closed my eyes and waited for death . . .

But it never came. There was a horrible sucking sound like a hoover swallowing a pile of crisp crumbs, and then . . . nothing! Everything stopped. There was absolute silence. It felt like we were indoors now. I was about to take a peak when . . .

'Keep your eyes shut!' I heard Brimstone whisper, except this time his voice was close. Really close. As though he was inside my head! 'I've decided to help you after all.'

And then another voice, a gentle one, warm like honey, whispered softly in my ear: 'Oh, heavens . . . how awful . . . are you hurt, young man?'

'SAY NOTHING!' hissed Brimstone from deep inside my brain.

Then the honey voice spoke again. 'Do you need some help? Are you, perhaps, lost?'

Of course, what I wanted to do was shout, *Yes!*

I am lost, actually. There's been a terrible mix up, and somehow I got bundled up in this blanket and I'd quite like to go home now! But I couldn't. My mouth felt like it had actually forgotten how to move. Was Brimstone controlling me? Maybe he was a telepathic reptile with the strange ability to paralyse my gob!

'Tell her your name is Thomas Kirk and that your father sent you to return her blanket.'

What?

'Tell her,' insisted Brimstone from inside my head. 'It's your only chance!'

'Er . . . my name is Thomas Kirk,' I mumbled, still keeping my eyes shut. 'And my dad sent me to return your blanket . . .'

'And why would he do that?' The voice had changed now, suddenly ice cold.

'Tell her that your dad is Jimmy Kirk and he knew she'd like it back.'

I couldn't imagine why he wanted me to say that. But I told her.

There was a pause, and a slight gnashing sound. Then I heard Brimstone whisper, 'She's put her glasses on, you can look now.'

Cautiously, I lifted my head a few centimetres and spotted the witch's shoes. They were dark red – blood red – with sharp, pointy heels that reminded me of commando-style stiletto knives, the type an action hero would keep tucked inside his pants in case of trouble.

'Welcome to Lower Spit Lighthouse,' said the voice, warm like honey again. 'My name is Pallidia Black.' And then a cold hand, with scratchy nails, reached for mine and pulled me to my feet.

CHAPTER 5

She didn't look like a witch. Or a lighthouse keeper. She looked like a rock star or a scary biker chick. She was quite young, not at all warty. And she wasn't wearing a black frock and pointy hat either. She wore tight, black leather trousers, a frilly black shirt, and huge pop-star sunglasses that blacked out her eyes. Her hair was the colour of coal and reached down to her waist. It was big and wild, like someone in a shampoo advert. And when she turned her head I spotted a strange tattoo down one cheek; a green serpent that glistened when she moved.

Her wrists were covered in jangly charm bracelets. And a black locket hung from her neck. But it was her lips that were the most disturbing. They were a dark purply red colour. Not like lipstick. It looked like she'd

been sucking raw steak. I felt the hairs on my arms
bristle like porcupines.

'Well,' she purred, her breath hot and strange-
smelling, 'I can certainly see the family resemblance.
You have your father's eyes . . .'

I blinked self-consciously, feeling like
a specimen in a jar. She ran a bony
finger down my cheek, and I
shivered. Then she turned away
to examine the blanket.
I saw her pluck a
small feather from
inside it, which
she shoved in her
back pocket.

'So you brought it home, did you? Well, that's kind . . .' As she touched the blanket it wriggled like a cat being stroked. 'Have you missed me?' she purred. Then she looked up sharply. 'You didn't find an annoying little reptile with it?'

'No!' whimpered Brimstone, from inside my skull. 'Don't tell her!'

I shook my head.

'Pity,' she murmured. 'Though I'm sure he'll turn up sooner or later. They always do!' She stood up. 'But the question is – what shall I do with you, Thomas Kirk? You see, while I'd love to sit and chat, I'm expecting company . . .'

'Visitors?' I said, glancing around nervously. We were in a small room, like the top of a turret. The giant lamp was in the middle, which thankfully she'd now turned off. 'Are they lighthouse keepers like you?'

'Ha!' she cackled, sounding for the first time quite witchy. 'Lighthouse keepers!'

I smiled too, trying to share the joke, which I didn't understand. But my smile disappeared as Brimstone whispered, 'She's going to kill you! You need to do something, quick!'

I took a step backwards, and bumped into the lamp. What could I do? There was nowhere to run. Nowhere to hide.

'I've got a plan,' whispered Brimstone. 'Do exactly as I say. Tell her your dad's coming to collect you, but while you're waiting you'll be happy to fix any gadgets that are broken.'

What? How would that help? Besides, I couldn't fix anything even if I wanted to. I'm nothing like my dad.

'Tell her! Or you're toast!' growled Brimstone. 'She'll only let you live if she thinks you'll be useful to her.'

I gulped. Then I took a deep breath. 'Er . . . do you have anything that needs fixing, I mean, while I'm here? I've got a bit of time before my dad arrives . . . he's coming to collect me, you see, by er . . . motorboat?'

'Really?' she said. 'Motorboat? I don't remember Jimmy owning a motorboat.'

I was beginning to wonder if my dad had some sort of secret life he hadn't told me about.

Pallidia Black folded her arms and tapped her long red nails against her skin. 'Well, perhaps there are a few tasks you could do for me. If you look like your father, perhaps you can fix like him, too.' Then suddenly she reached over and grabbed my chin, twisting my face up to hers. 'I wonder what colour you would be, Thomas?' She squeezed tighter, like I was a tube of toothpaste, making me wince. 'Young people are always so wonderfully . . . *shiny.*'

My belly lurched. And I felt a horribly squirmy sensation. Like Hansel and Gretel must have felt when they spotted the witch's oven!

'Perhaps I'll find out later . . .' she said, releasing me. 'But for now, follow me . . . oh, and be a pet, roll up the Cruiser and bring it along with you.'

But the blanket didn't need my help; immediately it rolled itself up. I hoisted it on to my shoulder, sailor style, and reluctantly followed Pallidia out of the lamp room into the stairwell.

It was narrow and dark out there. And the steps twisted tightly round in a downward spiral. Pictures covered the walls. Old-fashioned people in strange clothes and hats gazed out gloomily from their frames, their eyes following me as I passed by. One of them, a young woman in a white apron, seemed to lurch towards me, reaching out . . .

'Come along,' snapped Pallidia. 'Don't dawdle!' At the sound of her voice, the picture of the woman instantly froze, her arms still outstretched.

I decided not to look at any of the others. But I could feel their eyes on my back as I scuttled past.

The steps led down to another room, slighty larger than the one above and stuffed with dead animals. Rabbits, foxes, squirrels and some exotic creatures too – a tiger cub, a lioness, a crocodile; its mouth propped open in a ghoulish grin. All were displayed in glass specimen cases, like you find in a museum.

'Her trophies,' whispered Brimstone from inside my head.

Pallidia swept past them without a glance. But I couldn't help staring. They all had such ghastly expressions.

The next flight of stairs was brighter, lit by dozens of small jars strung along the wall like fairy lights. Each one was a different colour, a rainbow glow in the darkness. I felt my spirits lift at the sight.

'You wouldn't like them if you knew what they were,' Brimstone muttered. And again I wondered if he was reading my mind.

The room below was larger still, and full of ornaments. I hate rooms like that. I always think I'm going to break something. I tiptoed carefully past tables and cabinets and dusty shelves packed with little glass sculptures and dainty china ornaments. Then I spotted a shelf full of snow globes, the things my nan buys when she goes to the seaside. 'Greetings from Middle Spit Sands' was written at the bottom of a large one near the front. Inside was a Punch and Judy tent, with the little puppets on stage and the puppeteer's face peeking out from behind. Another snow globe contained a sad-looking waitress, clutching a tray of cream cakes.

'Delightful, aren't they,' said Pallidia, reaching past me to snatch it up. She shook it violently and a blizzard erupted. As Pallidia replaced the globe, I noticed the waitress inside looked even sadder than before. Her face streaked with tears.

Pallidia's eyes sparkled. 'She looks so real, doesn't she . . .'

'Bad witch,' growled Brimstone. 'Very bad witch!' He spoke so loudly that for a second I thought Pallidia might have heard him through my ear hole!

But she hadn't. She swept out of the room, and we were off again. Down more stairs, through more rooms. I gave up looking at the oddities they contained. Garden gnomes, gargoyles, clothes-shop dummies, endless photographs and paintings, old trunks, boxes and cabinets. And everywhere those jars with the flickering coloured lights . . . until finally we reached a large hall at the bottom of the lighthouse, which had several doors leading off it.

'The kitchen!' said Pallidia, throwing open the largest door. A cloud of dampness drifted out, enveloping me in fog. My clothes instantly felt wet and the smell of mould and decay was overpowering. Pallidia shoved me inside. The floor was slippery and I skidded into the centre of the room. I gasped. Everything was green. The table, the chairs, the cooker and all the surfaces. Even the floor, walls and ceiling were green. Not because they were painted that colour, but because they were covered in a thick wet moss.

'Sea lichen,' grinned Pallidia, running a finger along the table and licking it. 'Delicious. And so good for the complexion. Don't you think I look young and beautiful, Thomas?' She smiled like a crocodile.

'Er . . . yeah,' I stammered.

'Ha!' she cackled. Then she threw open a tall cupboard and hauled out an old vacuum cleaner. 'This doesn't work,' she said, dumping it at my feet.

I gulped. Now was definitely not the time to tell her that I didn't have a clue how to plug it in, let alone fix it.

'It's a dream cleaner,' she said, prodding it with the pointy toe of her shoe. 'But it doesn't make good dreams any more. Fix it!'

'Sure,' I said, laying down the electric blanket so I could pretend to take a proper look. 'It's probably, just the . . . er . . . sprockets that have gone . . .'

Pallidia shrugged then glanced at her watch. 'I need to rest before my visitors arrive. I'll return in one hour.' Then she swept out of the kitchen, locking the door behind her.

CHAPTER 6

'Brimstone?' I hissed, 'Where are you? Come out! You've got to help me!' I poked the blanket, wondering if that's where he was hiding. But just then I felt a sudden itch in my left ear and a tiny worm shot out and landed in my lap.

'Urgh, gross!' I yelped, flicking the maggot away, but as I did, something weird happened. It shook and wiggled and then burst into . . .

'Brimstone!' I leapt backwards, dropping the chameleon on the ground. 'How . . . what? Hey! Were you inside my ear?'

'Yes,' said the chameleon. 'It was the only place she wouldn't find me.'

'That's foul! What sort of a lizard *are* you?'

'I told you,' boggled the chameleon. 'I'm an

Antarctic chameleon. I was born in a volcano on the Deception Islands.'

'That doesn't explain how you can burrow into my brain. Or talk!'

Brimstone flicked out his tongue to catch a passing fly. 'Volcanic chameleons are special. We don't just change colour, we can change shape too.'

I frowned. 'Look, that's impossible. I watch hundreds of wildlife programmes – they're Dad's favourite – and I've never seen anything about a chameleon that can change shape!'

'I'm extinct,' said Brimstone sadly. 'I was the last of my kind. That's why Pallidia made me her familiar. Because I'm special.'

'What?'

'She made me her familiar. Her assistant. She enchanted me so I could talk. I've been her slave ever since. But then two weeks ago I managed to escape in the Snooze Cruiser when old Bladderwart – the witch who brought it to your shop – stole it from Pallidia!'

I groaned. 'And then I triggered the homing device and brought you back again.' I scuffed the mossy floor with my foot. 'I'm sorry.'

'Doesn't matter . . . we're both stuck here now. Welcome to the Lighthouse of Souls, our prison for eternity.'

I looked at him blankly. 'I don't understand . . .'

'Pallidia Black is a siren soul-taker, a witch of the darkest kind – she steals souls!'

I felt my throat tighten. 'How?'

'With her eyes,' whispered Brimstone, 'That's why I told you not to look at them. She hypnotises people with her eyes, then sucks out their souls with her monstrous breath. Then she traps them inside something – a box, a jar, a bottle – anything that takes her fancy . . .'

'Weird!'

'The snake on her cheek was a soul she sucked out. Only she forgot to blow it back out and trap it in something. Now it's stuck inside *her* for ever. And those little jars you saw that light up the stairs . . . each one contains the soul of a child.'

'That's terrible!'

Brimstone nodded. 'She stole a whole troop of Austrian scouts once. And then there was the junior orchestra from a school in Switzerland. Oh, and hundreds of brownies and guides . . .'

'And the pictures?'

Brimstone's eyes boggled. 'Sometimes she traps her victims in a photograph of themselves.'

I felt a lurch in my belly as I remembered the woman who had reached out to me. 'And what about the stuffed animals? And the snow globes?'

'Everything in the lighthouse has a soul trapped inside . . . though not all the souls are trapped. She allows some to float free.'

'What? In here? Where?' I looked around the moss-covered kitchen.

'Don't stare. It scares them.'

I looked again, but still couldn't see anything.

'They're everywhere, Tom.'

And then I saw one. A pale shape pressed into the corner of the ceiling, like a transparent gargoyle, staring back at me anxiously. Then I spotted another, lurking behind the vacuum cleaner – it didn't appear to have much of a body, but its face was large and balloon-like with enormous gloomy eyes.

'If they're free to go,' I whispered, 'why can't they just escape?'

'Where to?' Brimstone sighed. 'When you take

someone's soul, their body doesn't last long. Some of these souls were taken almost a century ago . . . they have nothing to return to.'

'That's horrible.'

Brimstone nodded. 'But she wasn't always like this, you know . . . Pallidia used to be an ordinary witch – a stitch witch, the helpful sort – until one day her world was turned upside down, and she did something so bad that her dark side took over and her heart turned to stone . . .'

I grimaced. 'Are there others like her?'

'Pallidia belongs to a ghastly coven – they call themselves the Soul Traders. They meet a few times each year to gossip and swap souls. They're always trying to outdo each other with the most exciting ways to display the souls they steal. One time it was doorknobs. The next it was gargoyles. Then garden gnomes – they stuffed little plaster gnomes with the souls of old men they stole from golf courses and bowling greens. Then they sold them to garden centres. It was their little joke. Perhaps you have one in your garden . . .'

As Brimstone spoke, I saw another soul, a tiny one, slip out from under the fridge door, followed by two more. The peered up at me with anxious eyes. I reached out to them, and instantly they vanished.

'They're afraid of you,' Brimstone whispered. 'They fear you're a spy.'

'I don't believe this!' I leant back, shaking my head. 'This coven,' I whispered. 'Are they the visitors Pallidia is expecting?'

'Probably. Not many other people come here willingly.'

'My dad's not one of them, is he?' I said anxiously. Ever since Pallidia had mentioned that she knew my dad, I'd had a horrible feeling he was up to his neck in bad stuff.

'Of course not!' Brimstone boggled me crossly. 'Jimmy Kirk hasn't set foot here in twenty years. He did come once, but as soon as he realised what sort of a witch Pallidia was, he never came back. Your father only helps good witches.'

I frowned. 'He actually came to this lighthouse?' I couldn't quite imagine Dad mending Pallidia's washing machine or fixing her telly.

'Don't you know who your father is, Thomas? He's a handyman to the dark side. Cauldrons, broomsticks, para-capes, moon spoons, foot knots, wands . . . he can fix anything.'

My brain boggled. Moon spoons? Para-capes? 'That's ridiculous! He's just a normal bloke. And anyway,' I said firmly, 'why can't people like Pallidia fix things themselves? With magic!'

Brimstone shrugged. 'Most witches specialise. They tend to be good at one thing. Whether it's changing the weather . . . or making gold . . .' He shuddered. 'Or taking souls. They stick to what they know. And for everything else they find other people. Just like humans.'

'So that's why Gloria brought Dad the Snooze Cruiser?'

'Yes. But she broke his rule. She came during the day on a Saturday, which your father forbids! Most of his customers come at night . . . and never at weekends.'

'Which is why I never see them.'

'Exactly. But Gloria's a bit dim. She's a stench witch who specialises in making bad smells. Not the brightest specimen. If she was, she would never have stolen the Snooze Cruiser from Pallidia. But she spotted it at a gathering of witches in Edinburgh two weeks ago and pinched it when Pallidia's back was turned. Then of course the blanket wouldn't work for her.'

'Which is why she brought it to Dad . . . and then it brought us here.' I got to my feet and began pacing the kitchen. 'And now *somehow* we've got to get out of here. There must be another way out. Maybe we can swim ashore.' I glanced at my watch – it was barely three o'clock. There was hours of daylight left. Plenty of time to escape.

'Impossible! The rocks are full of traps and enchantments. And even if you made it through them, there are the gannet ghouls to deal with. Fiendish, flesh-eating, zombie birds who'd peck your eyes out the moment you set foot outside.'

I collapsed next to the vacuum cleaner. 'Then we're stuck here for ever!' I puffed out my cheeks with frustration. 'And it's not as though I can fix anything. I don't know the first thing about vacuum cleaners!'

'It's not a vacuum cleaner. It's a *dream* cleaner. It sucks up the bad stuff – dirt, dust, doom, gloom – and turns it into nice dream clouds that burst over you when you're asleep.'

'And it doesn't work any more?'

'It's clogged up with lost souls,' said Brimstone, glumly. 'And they don't make for peaceful dreams.'

I picked up the machine and looked down the mouth of the sucking pipe. Dozens of eyes blinked back at me from the dark. I dropped it with a gasp. 'Well I don't want to end up like them. Come on, Brimstone, let's make a run for it . . .'

'Noooooooooooo!' Came a dozen whispers from round the room.

'What?'

'Don't gooooooo!' whispered the voices. 'She'll get yooooooouuuuuu . . .'

'They're right,' said Brimstone. 'You might as well accept your fate.'

Just then I heard a shout outside. It sounded like a girl's voice. 'Hello! Hello? Anyone at home?'

I dragged a chair over to the high window and clambered up. She was small, about my age, with bright-red hair tied in plaits. And she was steering a boat carefully between the rocks around the bottom of the lighthouse. The sea was calm, but even so she was being buffeted wildly. And every time she got close to the reef, another wave sent her crashing back again.

'Fool!' whispered Brimstone, who had scuttled up

the wall and was now sitting on the window ledge next to me. 'Those rocks have sunk a thousand ships!'

I banged on the window and waved to her. 'Go away,' I called. 'This place is dangerous!'

'She's not here,' I fibbed. 'Go away!' *Escape while you can*, I thought glumly.

As I spoke, I saw a dark shadow pass above the girl. I craned my neck. A flock of seabirds was hovering above her.

'The gannet ghouls,' I whispered. 'Go away!' I yelled again, banging even more loudly on the glass. But she continued to wave and shout. And then I had a thought. Perhaps she could fetch help . . .

'Wait!' I yelled. 'Listen! I'm being held prisoner here. My name is Thomas Kirk. Go home and call the police . . . and my dad, too! His name is Jimmy Kirk. He's got a repair shop in Weaverton. Please – go back and get help. Quickly!'

But the girl wasn't looking at me any more. She'd spotted someone on the other side of the lighthouse, a person who I couldn't see from my window. She was waving and smiling at the person. And then a terrible thing happened. A thick rope was flung to the girl, which she attached to her boat. And then it began to be pulled in towards the reef.

'No,' I gasped. 'Get away!' But it was too late. The boat had disappeared around the side of the lighthouse.

Brimstone sighed. 'I think the Lighthouse of Souls has a new inmate,' he said.

CHAPTER 7

A few minutes later we heard footsteps and raised voices. Brimstone scuttled off into the shadows just as the kitchen door burst open and Pallidia Black stood in the doorway, her hair wild, her face flushed. In one hand she held a piece of scrunched-up paper. In the other, the hood of a small, wriggling girl, her wild red plaits jiggling as she tried to escape the witch's clutches.

'But you don't understand, Miss Black,' she was squealing. 'I wasn't trespassing; I was dropping off an invite to our bingo night . . .'

'Silence,' the witch hissed. And the serpent on her cheek writhed angrily. 'I will not be interrupted when I'm resting.' She threw the girl roughly into the room, followed by the scrunched up paper. 'And what about you?' she glared at me. 'Have you fixed that wretched thing yet?' She kicked the dream cleaner, and the souls inside groaned.

'Er . . . I was just about to.'

'Well, if you need any spare parts,' glowered the witch. 'Feel free to use that piece of junk!' She gave the Snooze Cruiser a kick too. And there was a sudden high-pitched mew, much like the noise a kitten makes. 'The rotten traitor allowed itself to be stolen,' snarled Pallidia. 'So I won't trust it again!' She turned to go, but then stopped and sniffed the air. 'What's that smell?' She spun on her heel, glaring around the room. 'Reptilian blood,' she spat. 'Brimstone! Are you in here?'

'Oh, that pong is probably me,' said the red-haired girl cheerfully. 'I was trying out the new perfume range from Mr Blair's shop. He's the grocer in our town . . .' she added for my benefit. 'It's Turtle Spit – want to sniff?' she offered her neck to the witch.

Pallidia's eyes narrowed. Then she stormed out of the room, slamming the door behind her.

'It's okay, you can come out now,' whispered the girl, as a small brown rat poked its nose from underneath the tall cupboard, then morphed back into Brimstone.

'Who are you?' I gasped. 'And how did you know about Brimstone?'

'My name's Ruby Button. And everyone knows about him . . . well, everyone who reads the *Darkington Times*.'

'The what?'

'It's a newspaper for witches,' said Ruby. 'There was a story in it about Pallidia having her blanket and familiar stolen.'

'So you're a witch too?' I groaned. That was all I needed.

'No.' Ruby's face reddened. 'But I wish I was. My best friend's mother is a witch, which means one day he'll probably be one too . . . not that he's particularly excited by the prospect,' she added gloomily. 'But I don't have any witchy folk in my family.'

'Maybe that's a good thing.' I picked up the crumpled-up piece of paper and smoothed it out.

BINGO NIGHT!
EYES DOWN FOR MAGIC
AND MISCHIEF AT THE
POISONED KETTLE CAFÉ,
SCREAMING SANDS,
MONDAYS AT 7pm.

I handed it back to her. 'Sounds great,' I said unconvincingly.

She made a face. 'It's not a real bingo night. I made it up. It was just an excuse to meet her.'

'Who? Pallidia Black?' At the mention of her name, the lost souls in the room groaned. 'You're mad!'

But Ruby wasn't listening. She was looking around the room. 'I can see them, you know,' she whispered. 'The lost souls, I mean. There are dozens in here, aren't there . . .' She gave them a wave. 'Hello . . . nice to meet you . . . I'm Ruby!' She smiled at me. 'This place is exactly as they said it would be . . .'

'Who?'

'The O'Hara sisters – three old banshees who stayed in our town last year. They told me all about the Lighthouse of Souls, and Pallidia Black! The O'Hara sisters are old friends of hers, you know.'

My head was swimming, what with witches and banshees and bingo nights. 'But why would you want to come here when you know what goes on?'

'Because I was hoping Pallidia might take me on as her assistant!'

'What?' It was Brimstone's turn to be shocked. 'Why?'

'Because she's such a powerful witch, of course. I was hoping she might teach me a thing or two.'

'You want to be like her?' I shook my head confused. 'You're bonkers!'

'It's all right for you, Thomas Kirk,' said Ruby poking my shop badge with a bony finger. 'I know who you are. I know all about your family's connections with the dark side. I see your dad's adverts in the *Darkington Times*. But for the rest of us it's much harder to move in magic circles.'

'What? You're *jealous* of me?' I stared at her incredulously. 'You're even madder than Pallidia!' I got to my feet and walked over to the window. 'Personally I don't want to have anything to do with the dark side, thanks very much. I just want to go home.'

As I spoke, I saw the dark shadow of the gannets pass over the reef, momentarily darkening the sky. I shivered. Night would be coming soon, and with it Pallidia's guests. I just hoped I wasn't part of the evening's entertainment.

CHAPTER 8

'The woman lives on pilchards!' wailed Ruby as she opened a cupboard and found it full of tinned fish. 'And there's not even a can opener!' She slammed the cupboard shut, scaring a lost soul who'd been snoozing at the back. Ruby's excitement at meeting her hero had subsided a bit, only to be replaced by hunger.

'Stop complaining and help me,' I snapped. I was on my hands and knees now, tapping the flagstones. 'There's always a trap door in the movies . . . maybe there's a false stone that leads to an underground tunnel . . .'

'But where would it lead?' Ruby scowled at me. 'Use your brains, Thomas. It would take you straight into the sea. And in case you haven't noticed, there's a force-ten gale blowing out there!'

Of course I'd noticed. The sea was crashing around us, lashing at the window like an iron whip. The wind was howling too. And the souls were moaning along with it. It was like being trapped on the set of a musical horror film.

I started patting the stones again.

'Be careful,' said Brimstone gloomily. 'You might hit the witch brick!'

'The what?'

'Lighthouse architects were a superstitious breed. They always fitted their lighthouses with a lynch-pin safety brick, so if the lighthouse fell into the wrong hands – witch hands – it could be collapsed in an instant.'

I raised my eyebrows. 'That's too silly to be true!'

Brimstone boggled me crossly. 'Well it is. The witch brick is said to be red. There's one in every lighthouse if you look. But if you find it, be careful not to loosen it, or the whole place might come tumbling down on your head!'

'More pilchards,' grumbled Ruby, banging yet another cupboard.

I was losing patience with them both. 'If only you'd

called the police when I asked,' I said to Ruby, 'then we'd all be home by now.' I looked at my watch. It was eight o'clock. My parents would be going nuts. 'Won't your family be worried?' I asked Ruby.

She shrugged. 'They don't know I'm here. Dad's on tour again – he's in a heavy metal band. And Mum thinks I'm at scout camp.'

'Well won't the scout leader be worried if you don't turn up?'

'Nah, I had everything planned. I called the leader yesterday pretending to be my mum. I told them I was sick and wasn't coming.'

'Great,' I groaned.

'Yep – then I stole a boat,' added Ruby cheerfully. 'Or rather, I borrowed one off Mrs Hunter's brother, Jock. He helps Mrs Hunter in the hotel at Screaming Sands . . .'

'Where?'

'Screaming Sands! It's a town a few miles up the coast. It's actually called Middle Spit Sands, but me and my friend Davie renamed it when we turned it into a ghost town.'

I frowned. Maybe it was tiredness, but I was

struggling to keep up. Things were getting weirder and weirder.

'I'll tell you the story one day. It's an amazing place,' said Ruby, her eyes glowing. 'It's where folk from the dark side spend their holidays. Witches, vampires, the undead – you'd love it!'

'Er . . . maybe,' I said politely.

'It's got an amazing ice-cream parlour too, and a zombie donkey.'

'Well, anywhere would be better than here,' I said, moving the blanket to check the flagstones underneath it. As I did, the blanket gave a little squeak.

'It seems to like you,' said Brimstone. 'It doesn't normally talk.'

Talking blankets – I'd heard it all now. I felt around the last few stones. Nothing.

'Brimstone,' I said desperately. 'Can't you just shrink yourself into something small, like a flea or something, and slip under the door and go and find a key.'

But before he could reply there was a flash of light outside the window. For a second I thought it might be a coastguard's boat come to rescue us. I raced over to look.

'Blooming 'eck!' muttered Ruby, squashing on to the chair next to me. 'Looks like she's got company!'

The light I'd seen was the beam of the lighthouse. It was rotating slowly, illuminating large chunks of the sky. As it flashed round, several sinister shadows were picked out. They looked like moths, flying through the air towards us.

'Who are they?' I asked.

'The creatures you meet in nightmares,' groaned Brimstone. 'Only much scarier.'

As he spoke, the lost souls began to wail.

'I think I've changed my mind,' said Ruby in a small voice. 'Perhaps I won't be a soul taker's assistant, after all.' She hopped from foot to the other. 'And I think I need a wee!'

I was about to tell her to 'go' in the sink, when the lighthouse lamp suddenly disappeared. A moment later Brimstone gave a tiny shriek. 'She's coming!' And he vanished just as the door crashed open and Pallidia stalked in . . .

'What are you lot gawping at?' She glared at the lost souls, who shrank back into the shadows. Then she pointed a finger at me. 'The lighthouse lamp has broken. You must fix it!'

'What?' I swallowed hard. She must be kidding.

'You *can* fix things, can't you?'

Nope! Nothing! But I gave a nod, hoping the fib wouldn't show on my face.

'Come on then!' As she turned, she glanced at Ruby. 'Can you dance?'

Ruby blinked back at her for second, then shrugged. 'Well . . . er . . . not exactly,' she stammered, her face turning the same colour as her hair. 'You see, I sort of tried tap dancing once, but I stood on the teacher's toes and put my elbow in Shelley Dobb's face and cracked her specs and then . . .'

Pallidia held up her hand. 'Enough!' She turned to go, then stopped again and stood looking at the blanket for a few moments, her eyes narrowed. 'Bring that thing with you,' she said to me. 'Roger Pilkington-Smith might like it as a gift . . .'

Ruby gawped at me. '*Roger Pilkington-Smith?*' she mouthed silently, as though the name meant something to her. Then she grabbed an end of the blanket. 'I'll help you carry it, Tom.'

Pallidia looked like she was about to protest, but then her face softened and her voice turned to honey. 'Yes,' she purred. 'Do come along, dear, I'm sure someone will be interested in you, too . . .' She ran a long bony finger over Ruby's red plaits, like a fox checking out the belly of a chicken. I shivered. But Ruby didn't flinch. She was obviously made of tougher stuff. Then the witch turned and stalked out, and we followed her into the stairwell.

CHAPTER 9

The lighthouse looked different in the dark; a million times more terrifying. The only glow was from the tiny flickering lights. And now I knew they were the souls of lost children it was hard to look at them without a lurch in my belly. They cast human-shaped shadows across the walls, and their tiny voices whispered, 'Help me, save me,' as we passed by. It seemed that now I knew what horrors the lighthouse held, I was able to hear the lost souls that surrounded me. I was part of their secret world.

I put my head down and raced after Pallidia. My palms felt sweaty. My heart was thumping. At every level of the lighthouse, I expected to come face to face with Pallidia's guests. It was a relief to find each room empty.

But then we started to run out of landings and we reached the staircase that led to Pallidia's treasure room, and I knew that's where they would be waiting. I was right . . .

'What's this?' came a smooth voice, echoing down the stairs. 'Have you got new assistants, Pallidia?'

'Ha!' scoffed the witch.

As the stair curved into the room, I saw the owner of the voice. A tall thin man in a black shirt and trousers, with a super-shiny disco belt, which flashed and rippled and hurt my eyes when I looked at it.

Behind him was a bent old woman with a dark leathery face and a diamond nose ring that winked in the light. Next to her, two blonde witches, one older than the other; mother and daughter maybe, in matching grey suits. The older one had enormous ball-shaped earrings dangling from her lobes. There was something quite odd about them. And as I peered closer I realised what it was – they were covered in tiny ears that twitched and writhed.

On the other side of the room was a small round-faced man, sitting at a table. He was the only one of them not wearing dark glasses. But he wasn't interested in us. He was peering at a silver box that sat on the table in front of him.

'I can't sell her unless she dances,' he was grumbling, giving whatever was inside a poke.

'She'll dance,' shrieked Pallidia. 'Or else!'

There was the sound of music from the box and I moved closer to see inside. I caught a glimpse of a sullen-looking ballerina the size of my finger trapped inside a tiny glass dome at the back of the box. Her arms were folded and she had a sulky expression on her face.

'Roger will buy her even if she doesn't dance,' snapped Pallidia. 'He loves my treasures.'

'Or perhaps he'll want my minotaur instead,' said the man with the sparkly disco belt. He swept across the room and deposited a snow globe on the table. Inside, chained to a stump, was a human figure with a bull's head. I gulped. It looked like some mythical creature from ancient Greece. It was snorting angrily and pawing the ground with its tiny human foot. And then suddenly it charged. But it had nowhere to go. It hit the glass and bounced back, before collapsing to the ground in despair.

'Ha!' scoffed Pallidia. 'Smoke and mirrors! That's no minotaur – it's a man with a bull's head glued on!'

'Nonsense,' he said icily.

'He won't be interested in either,' said the leather-faced old lady, shoving them both aside. 'Not when he sees this!' She drew out a red velvet bag from under her cloak and tossed it on to the table, where it spilled open.

'Chess pieces?' I whispered.

Pallidia glared at me.

'Exquisite!' breathed the round-faced man as each piece lifted itself up and slid blindly across the table as though looking for its place on a chessboard.

'There's a real king's soul inside the king,' said the old woman smugly. 'A queen inside the queen . . . and a real knight and his horse trapped for ever in the rook . . .'

'Rubbish!' scoffed Pallidia.

'Are you calling me a liar?' The woman bared her teeth.

'I am!' Pallidia spat on the floor and the serpent on her cheek writhed angrily.

'Perhaps I should cut that creature out of your cheek,' offered the old lady, reaching for a knife that was poking out her boot. 'Or bite it out, if you prefer . . .'

'Ladies, ladies,' said the man at the table. 'Remember we have a customer coming. And Mr Pilkington-Smith won't buy anything if you squabble!'

'Well he won't come at all unless the boy can fix the light,' Pallidia snapped, poking me hard in the back. 'Come on!'

But the blonde woman barred our way. 'How can he fix it?' she demanded.

'He's a Kirk,' said Pallidia sharply. 'Jimmy Kirk's boy.'

There was a sharp intake of breath around the room, and then a few wolfish grins. Dad's name obviously meant something to them.

'Perhaps you'll take a look at this?' said the oily man in black. He tapped his middle. 'Orion's belt,' he said proudly. And his waistband sparkled like disco lights. But then one side went out. 'It keep's doing that,' he grumbled, giving it a thump.

'Real stars,' breathed Ruby. 'He must be a star taker!'

'Star faker, more like,' growled Pallidia.

'Seen one of these before?' demanded the old lady, dipping her head in front of my face. I gasped. There was a bloodshot eye fixed to the top of her head. It stared back at me like a dead fish.

'An all-seeing eye . . .' whispered Ruby.

'Yeah,' growled the granny. 'But it's got something stuck in it.'

As she spoke, the eye blinked grittily. Then closed completely.

'What about my ear spheres,' moaned the blonde witch, barging in front of the others. She cocked her head so her left earring swung a centimetre from my nose, making the little ears twitch and wriggle. 'One of them is hissing.'

I took a deep breath and looked more closely. Some ears were hairy. Most were waxy and one was definitely hissing.

'Ear spheres . . .' I heard Ruby mutter. 'So she can hear the snitch witch spies . . .'

'Enough, all of you,' snapped Pallidia. 'He hasn't got time to fix your ridiculous gadgets.' She grabbed my arm. 'He's got my lamp to mend.' And she dragged me roughly out of the room.

CHAPTER 10

'There it is – fix it!'

We were back in the lamp room now. Me, Pallidia and Ruby, with the blanket still rolled up between us. There were no lights up here, except for the big one, which was dead.

'Come on! What are you waiting for?'

I shivered in the darkness. Why hadn't I listened when Dad was prattling on about fixing stuff. Heck, I didn't even know how to change a plug – something Dad had been able to do when he was six!

'He doesn't have his tool box,' squeaked Ruby. 'Shall we pop back to his dad's shop to fetch it?'

Pallidia growled through the darkness. 'Fix it now, or I'll push you both into the sea!'

So I did something then that I'd seen my dad do

once. It was when he'd had the flu. He'd been laid up on the sofa watching snooker when the telly had gone on the blink. Instead of fetching his tool box, he'd got up, took off his slipper and whacked the telly with it. The picture instantly reappeared. 'Promise me, son,' he'd said with a serious expression on his face. 'Never do that unless you're in a sticky situation without a screw driver . . . okay?'

I reckoned this was exactly the sort of sticky situation he'd imagined. So I hauled off my trainer, and whacked the light as hard as I could.

Clunk!

For a second I wondered whether it might shatter! But it didn't. It flickered a bit, then burst into life, very nearly blinding us. Even the blanket didn't seem to like it, and gave a brief shriek.

'Ha!' shouted Pallidia. 'Thomas Kirk has made it work!' And she gave me a celebratory clatter on the back. For the second time that day I felt my teeth rattle in my skull. I hoped she wouldn't do it again. But just then there was a shout from the water down below, and Pallidia opened the window and leaned out, her face blasted with spray and wind.

'He's here,' she breathed. 'He's come by boat. I must go to him.' She shoved me aside and took off down the stairs, like a panther after its prey.

'I think our Pallidia's got the hots for Roger Pilkington-Smith,' giggled Ruby.

'Who?'

'Her guest. He's a ghastly man. An estate agent. Or he used to be. He tried to close down our town last year, but we got our revenge. A sackful of needle spiders and a visit from a ghostly bride did him in!'

'You mean, you killed him?' I frowned. 'Then how come he's here?'

'It's a long story . . . but the fact is you and I are in the smelly stuff. We've got to get out of here before she comes back.'

I peered out of the window. 'Maybe we could climb down and steal his boat?' I said, though I didn't really mean it. The lighthouse was at least twenty metres high, with smooth weather-washed walls and razor-sharp rocks waiting to skewer us at the bottom. Then I looked at the blanket. 'Or maybe we could fly away on that.'

'What?'

'It's a flying blanket,' I said, expecting Ruby to laugh. 'That's how I got here. It sort of attacked me, scooped me up and brought me here.'

'Genius!' Ruby immediately started unrolling it. But of course when we sat down on the thing nothing happened. No clunking. No clanking. Nothing.

'How do you get it to move?' Ruby shuffled her bottom, as though trying to encourage it to fly.

'Dunno!'

'What?' Ruby glared at me. 'But you said you could fly it!'

'I didn't.'

'Well how are we going to escape then? Oh, don't start that again!'

I was patting the blanket all over now, desperately searching for a control panel, or an 'ON' switch. And then I must have found it.

SHARRRROOOOM!

The front end of the electric blanket flipped up, followed by the back end, and then the whole thing began to vibrate and it lifted a few feet off the ground, where it hovered in the air as though waiting for instruction.

'Awesome!' breathed Ruby.

'Quick! Climb off and open the window,' I called, 'while I try to find the instruction manual. Brimstone said there was one . . .' Then I stopped. Brimstone. I'd forgotten about him. 'Ruby!' I gasped. 'We can't leave without Brimstone . . .'

'I'm here,' came a muffled voice, then his green face emerged through one of the corners of the blanket, just as before.

'You were in there all the time?'

He nodded. 'I thought it was the safest place to hide from Pallidia. And guess what? I found something useful.' He disappeared back into his invisible hole and reappeared with a small green booklet in his mouth. He dropped it at my feet. 'Instructions on how to fly the Snooze Cruiser!'

As I picked it up, the booklet expanded in my hand, becoming instantly fatter and heavier. I leafed through a couple of pages. The writing was tiny and the sentences all ran together without any gaps. It was total gobbledegook! I leafed through more pages, hoping to find a picture or a diagram. But there was nothing but text. Ant-sized tiny text.

Ruby meanwhile had clambered off the blanket, and was optimistically opening the window. An icy blast of wind burst into the room, making the pages of the book flutter wildly.

'There are more than 4,000 pages in this thing,' I groaned. 'Where do I start?'

'Dunno,' whispered Ruby, climbing back on to the blanket, 'but make it snappy, I think they're coming!'

She was right. I could hear footsteps on the staircase below. I slammed the booklet shut. 'Maybe I should just do the same thing I did last time,' I said flopping backwards. 'I just sort of lay down on the blanket like this . . .'

I didn't get a chance to finish, because the second my head hit the blanket there was a clunk and a clank and the blanket began to vibrate faster. Brimstone vanished into his hole again.

'Don't worry if the blanket suddenly smothers you,' I warned Ruby. 'That's how it takes off.'

But just then there was a horrible wail from the doorway.

'My Snooze Cruiser,' screamed Pallidia. 'Thieves!' She made a lunge for us, but too slow. The blanket didn't bother smothering us. It just shot out the window like a bullet. We were free . . .

But my relief vanished the second we got outside. The strong sea winds that I'd heard howling around the lighthouse were now raging around us. Ruby gave a yell as she was bounced across the blanket and very nearly fell off. 'Brimstone!' I shouted. 'We've got to find the air-shield lever!'

'I'm looking!'

I glanced up to see a small green snail slithering near the top of the blanket. He'd obviously morphed again. But just then there was a terrible *cack-cack-cack* sound. And above us a huge black shadow blotted out the moon.

'The gannets,' I heard Brimstone gasp.

And then I saw them – monstrous sea birds with enormous wings and dagger-like beaks, lining up above us like a formation of fighter pilots.

'Press the air-shield button.' I yelled to Brimstone.

But it was too late, they were coming . . .

CHAPTER 11

'Shut your eyes,' I shouted to Ruby. 'Or they'll peck them out!'

'What about the rest of me?' she wailed.

But the first bird was already dive-bombing down towards us like a rocket-propelled pterodactyl.

'Ruby,' I yelled. 'When I say "move", roll over to my side – the weight of us both should make the blanket tip up, and the bird might miss us!'

'What?'

'MOVE!' I screamed.

In the second it took for her to roll towards me, the beast was upon us. I felt a sudden sharp rip down one leg as its beak made contact, and then it shot past us. The unbalanced blanket tipped wildly and we both nearly fell off, but somehow we clung on until it righted itself.

'There's another one coming,' howled Ruby.

'Do it again!' I shouted back. 'When I say move . . .'

'Yeah, yeah,' she snapped. 'I've got it!'

But the second bird was wise to us. It slowed slightly, as though waiting for us to make our move, then got closer and closer before gravity kicked in and it increased its speed and dive bombed straight for us . . .

'MOVE!' I screamed.

But this time I didn't need to, because Brimstone had found the button. And just as the bird reached us, the air shield burst open and the bird bounced off, ricocheting away to oblivion!

'Geez,' breathed Ruby. 'I thought we were dead!'

'It's not over yet.' I peered up into the sky where the birds were massing again. 'They look like they're going to attack together . . . I hope this thing will hold!' I tapped the air shield. As I did, something fell from the air on to my lap.

'What the . . . ?'

Brimstone gave a shriek. 'The control panel!'

'What?'

'You found the control panel. Pallidia must have

hidden it up there – in the air shield. When you tapped it, you dislodged it.'

'Right,' I said, as though it was perfectly normal to hide a control panel in an invisible air shield! I gawped at the thing. It didn't look like any control panel I'd ever seen. It looked like the guts of some weird electrical gadget that had exploded and no one knew how to put back together. There were wires and knobs and levers and switches and dials and gauges, and all sorts of other weird things, but all put together in a totally random pattern. 'Is it supposed to look like this?'

Brimstone shrugged.

'Do something!' said Ruby, who was peering up at the birds.

I frowned. 'It's not exactly a remote-control car I'm trying to drive!'

Ruby made a face. 'Just give something a bit of a wiggle – look, what about that knob?' She twisted a large black dial and the blanket gave a horrible shudder. 'Er . . . maybe not.' Ruby twisted it back the other way, but instead of going faster, we began to bunny hop through the sky.

I grabbed another lever and pulled that. The bunny

hopping stopped, but so did the blanket. Completely! Then it flipped over and we all clunked our heads on the shield. I pulled the lever the *other* way and we turned the right way up, but then began to spin . . .

'Uh oh, here they come,' muttered Ruby. 'Look!'

Six of the monsters were banking up above us, getting into line, about to do a mass dive bomb.

I looked down at the panel. 'Come on,' I muttered. 'Help me!'

And then suddenly a red button lit up in the centre of the panel. A word was written on it . . .

'Tempus? What does that mean?'

'Time,' said Brimstone.

'How do you know stuff like that?' breathed Ruby.

Brimstone sniffed snootily. 'Being a familiar isn't just making cocoa and fetching slippers, you know.'

The button flashed again.

'I think it wants me to press it,' I said . . . but before anyone could reply there was a terrible crash! as the birds hit us. We dropped like a stone, spiralling down towards the sea.

'They've cracked the shield!' screamed Ruby, as one of the bird's beaks sliced through the invisible roof, just centimetres above our heads. Green slime oozed from its bill, and its eyes were the colour of blood.

Ruby glared at the creature. Then snatched off her shoe and smacked it hard across its beak.

Cack-cack-cack-cack, it honked crossly.

Then she did it again. Harder, this time. The bird pulled back its beak and darted off. Ruby grinned at me. 'You're not the only one who can fix things, Thomas Kirk.'

'Watch it,' called Brimstone, 'there's another group coming!'

I glanced up and saw another six birds dive bombing towards us. The button flashed again.

'Press it!' yelled Ruby. 'Quick!'

So I did.

And then everything turned blue. Ice blue. The wind stopped. We stopped. Even the birds stopped, suspended a metre above our heads, their beaks ready to batter more holes in the shield. And then another button lit up on the panel. A long rectangular one with numbers . . .

'I don't understand,' I frowned. 'Is it a code, or something?'

We all looked at it. And then Ruby's face lit up. 'It's the date,' she whispered. 'Today's date . . . and time. Look!'

'21:02, 02 06 12,' I read. Above and below the numbers were arrows. And then, suddenly, as though I'd been struck on the head with a frying pan, I understood exactly what the arrows were for. 'Brimstone,' I whispered. 'Can this blanket travel through time?'

He shrugged.

Ruby's mouth gaped open like a goldfish. 'Awesome!'

And for some reason, I was sure it could.

'So . . .' I said slowly. 'If the blanket can really travel through time, then we can go back to before any of this happened. Back to this morning, before Bladderwart even appeared in Dad's shop.'

Ruby cocked her head to one side. 'Who's Bladderwart?'

'. . . only this time,' I said, 'when she appears, I won't mess with the blanket. And then we won't end up at the Lighthouse of Souls. Right?'

'What about me?' Ruby made a face. 'I wasn't in your shop this morning!'

'Don't worry. Dad will take you home.'

'And what about me?' Brimstone asked nervously.

'You'll be free,' I grinned. 'Finally free. You can sneak out of the blanket before Bladderwart brings it to the shop. And then you can go and do whatever you want. Maybe we could even find you a boat back to the Deception Islands.'

'Do it!' yelled Ruby, glancing at the gannets. 'Who knows how long this frozen time thing will last – go on, Tom, change the time . . .'

I reached for the arrows, but something stopped me – a nagging thought in the back of my brain . . .

'But what about the others?' I said. 'The chess pieces, the snow globes . . . the little lights . . . the lost souls, Ruby! What about them?'

'We can't help them. But we *can* help ourselves. Go on, Tom, press the button, or I'll do it.'

'Brimstone,' I said. 'You told me Pallidia wasn't always bad. When did it happen? I mean when did she choose the dark side?'

'The evening of June 22nd, 1912,' said the chameleon. 'She sank a paddle steamer off the coast of Middle Spit Sands by turning off the lighthouse lamp. She was fifteen years old.'

'Who cares,' snapped Ruby. And she reached for the button. But I was faster. I snatched the control panel out of her reach and looked at Brimstone. 'What if we could change things . . . go back in time and stop Pallidia turning to the dark side. Then all those lost souls would be saved, wouldn't they?'

Brimstone boggled me but said nothing. I took one last look at the ghoul gannets and the lighthouse a little way off now, and then I did it. I changed the date. And time.

I saw a look of shock flash across Ruby's face. 'You're kidding, right?'

I didn't answer. I just shrugged. And then smiled. And then everything turned black.

CHAPTER 12

I felt like I was being electrocuted. There was a sudden intense feeling of heat. My hair shot up. My skin singed. And I could see all the bones in my body lit up like an X-ray. Then, just as suddenly, the heat vanished and I felt something cold wash over me, and I realised we were in the sea. The night had gone. The water was calm. And I was on my back, with the control panel still on my lap, floating on the blanket, which was now half submerged like a broken raft.

'Brimstone? Ruby?' My throat felt like sandpaper. I blinked in the sunshine and looked at my watch, but it was broken, the hands hanging limply like soggy shoelaces. I glanced round. Ruby was at the other end of the blanket, drifting away slightly. At the sound of her name she opened her eyes. 'What happened?'

'I'm not sure . . .'

She grinned. 'That was some ride!'

As she spoke, I noticed there were silver streaks down one side of her hair. I was about to tell her when she pointed her finger at my head and giggled.

'Hey, metal man, you should see yourself!'

'What?'

I ran my hand through my spiky hair and immediately got a static shock off it.

'The ends have turned silver,' she giggled.

'Yeah, well you're not exactly looking yourself, either.' Just then I felt something wriggle near my foot. A silver fish flapped past and Brimstone morphed back and landed on my shoulder. Even he had a slight silver sheen to his green body.

'I never want to do that again,' he said firmly.

'Where are we?' I tried to sit up, but as I did the blanket sank deeper into the water. Then Ruby gave a shout.

'Middle Spit Sands!'

'What?' I turned my head in the direction she was looking and saw a shingle cove looming in the distance. Behind it was a thin strip of sandy beach with a few dots on it – obviously people enjoying the sun. Beyond them was a small town.

'So it didn't work,' I said gloomily. 'We didn't go back in time.'

'Well look on the bright side,' said Ruby. 'At least the gannet ghouls didn't get us. And, hey, if we hadn't escaped from the lighthouse we'd be just another couple of sparkly jars sitting on a dusty shelf for ever.'

At the mention of the lighthouse, I turned round. There it was, far off in the distance, a tiny white peg on the horizon. It didn't look nearly so threatening in daylight, but even so I shivered. Maybe it was a good thing we hadn't gone back in time. I was hungry and tired and ready to go home.

'Help me paddle,' said Ruby, who was scooping water with her hands, trying to make the blanket move faster towards the shore.

'Er . . . Ruby, do the people in your town always dress so weirdly.'

'What?' She glanced up and scanned the beach. We were drifting closer now, and the people were clearer. They looked strangely old-fashioned – women in long skirts with wide-brimmed hats and men in caps with loopy droopy moustaches. Even the children looked odd, wearing long bathing bloomers that I wouldn't have been seen dead in – when I was five!

'I told you, Tom – Middle Spit Sands is the holiday destination of the dead,' said Ruby, who'd started paddling again. 'Some of them may look a little freaky, but they're really nice when you get to know them.'

However something didn't look right. The people didn't look dead, just different . . .

'Hey, you didn't tell me there was a roller coaster in Middle Spit Sands!'

'What?' Ruby stopped paddling and peered at the beach.

At the far end, just behind a row of coloured beach huts, was a rickety-looking wooden ride, where a single carriage was bumping its way up and down a track.

Ruby gawped. 'There *isn't* a roller coaster in our town . . .'

'Then where are we?'

'Middle Spit Sands . . .' said Brimstone '. . . a century ago!'

'What?' Ruby stood up to get a better look, and nearly sunk us.

'It's not a roller coaster, it's a switchback railway,' sniffed Brimstone. 'One of the first of its kind, but it burnt down the day Pallidia sank that paddle steamer.'

'Then it's worked,' I whispered. 'We've gone back in time.' And the people weren't weird, they were just from another century. My heart beat faster and I felt a twist in my tummy. I couldn't stop staring at them – their unfamiliar outfits, their funny hats – they were like the cast of some historical movie. These people had never seen the telly. Or the internet. Or an Xbox. Heck, they probably still thought the moon was made of cheese. Well . . . maybe not. Maybe they weren't quite that mad . . .

As we watched, more people arrived. Groups of children were building sandcastles and splashing in the water. Others were gathering to watch an old-fashioned Punch and Judy show. A few grown-ups were sitting on deck chairs, while others strolled along the front. They were doing all the usual stuff you do at the seaside, just wearing unusual outfits while they did it!

'So what's the plan?' Ruby suddenly gave me a hard look. 'What are we doing here, Tom?'

'We're going to stop Pallidia from sinking that paddle steamer.' My cheeks reddened. It sounded a bit silly now we were here.

Ruby's eyes bored into me. 'How?'

'I dunno . . .' I searched around for some sort of plan. Then I looked at Brimstone. 'Maybe you could tell us what happened. How Pallidia turned bad and why . . . and then maybe we'll think of something . . .'

The chameleon's eyes whizzed round nervously. And his tongue flicked in and out three times. Then he nodded and began to tell the story of how Palllidia Black turned to the dark side.

'Her family were famous stitch withes. They used their magic for sewing. Pallidia had six sisters and they all worked together in the family's tailoring business, making suits and jackets and frocks and hats. Pallidia was the most skilled. She was such a powerful witch, you see, even when she was young. She sewed invisibly. She could cut clothes with her mind. And she had such a good eye for detail. One customer – a sailor – was so taken with the suit Pallidia made for him, that he gave her a special pet . . .'

'What was that?' asked Ruby.

'It was a strange creature from a land far away, which the sailor had found on one of his voyages,' said Brimstone. 'Pallidia kept it with her always. She was devoted to it.'

'Oh, I felt like that about Winston, my gerbil,' interrupted Ruby. 'I had him when we were on tour with my dad's band. I kept him in the tour bus. But then one holiday, my nan's cat got him . . .'

'Shut up, Rubes,' I frowned. 'Go on, Brimstone.'

'Well, Pallidia and the creature were inseparable. It sat by her side while she sewed. It slept in her room at night. The only time they were apart was when Pallidia was out delivering sewing work. But then one day a terrible thing happened. Pallidia was away and a customer came into the shop, saw the creature and wanted it. Of course Pallidia's parents wouldn't part with it, but when their backs were turned, he took it . . .'

'What? Poor Pallidia,' gasped Ruby. 'That's awful!'

'It was,' said Brimstone. 'When Pallidia returned and found the creature gone, she flew into a rage. An angry witch is always bad, but Pallidia was on the cusp . . .'

'Ooooh,' breathed Ruby. 'That's dangerous!'

'What's the cusp?'

Ruby gave me a patronising look, as though I was more stupid than a particularly dim pigeon. 'Witches normally come into their powers when they're twelve, Thomas,' she said impatiently. 'Then they have a few years to get used to them, play around with them a bit, before deciding what sort of magic to specialise in.

They have to decide just before the summer solstice of their sixteenth year . . .'

'You mean like choosing what sort of job you want when you grow up?' I asked.

Ruby nodded. 'They choose what magic they want to study – a light art, something useful and helpful . . .'

'Like sewing?'

She nodded.

'Or a dark art,' I whispered. 'Like soul taking!'

'Exactly,' said Ruby. 'Powerful witches tend to opt for the dark side, because it's so much more exciting.' She winked at me mischievously.

'What about Pallidia?' I asked Brimstone. 'What path was she choosing?'

'Stitch witchery, of course. Until her creature – the one thing in the world she loved – was cruelly snatched from under her nose. Then her dark side reared up. She demanded to know who had taken it. And her parents told her. Septimus Silverback, the captain of a paddle steamer, the *SS Louisa*, which was sailing from Sunny Bay later that evening.'

Ruby nudged me. 'Sunny Bay is a town up the coast,' she whispered.

Brimstone boggled her crossly for interrupting again. 'Pallidia was in a terrible rage now – the shop shelves rattled, the ceiling cracked and the floorboards bowed beneath her. As she stormed out of the shop, the sky turned black. Her dark energies were rousing a storm – thunder boomed and bolts of lightning flew from her fingertips. One hit the switchback railway and set it alight. Not that Pallidia cared. She had stolen a boat by this time, and was rowing out to the lighthouse. She knocked out the keeper with a lightning blow to the head, and set him adrift in his boat. Then she waited in the lamp room until she saw the SS *Louisa* in the distance. She knew it would have to pass the needles – the dangerous rocks just beyond the lighthouse, and with the storm raging and waves the size of skyscrapers crashing around it, it would need the lighthouse to guide it past the rocks. Then just at the last moment, she turned off the light!'

'And the ship hit a rock,' I whispered, 'and sank?'

Brimstone nodded.

'And the creature?' asked Ruby. 'Did it drown?'

'No, but Pallidia didn't know that at the time. She rowed out to the ship as it began to sink, hoping to find her beloved. But there was no sign of him anywhere. She saw the captain, though. He and his passengers were escaping in lifeboats. She reared up and fixed the captain with such a terrible glare that she snatched his soul right from him, even before she knew she could take souls. She breathed it into the locket that she wears round her neck, then she sank the lifeboats and everyone drowned.

'And the creature?' Ruby frowned. 'Why didn't it drown, too?'

'Because it had an unusual ability to survive,' said Brimstone. 'It stuck itself to a broken timber and got washed up many miles away. Another witch found it and eventually Pallidia got her pet back . . . but she didn't know that then . . . her heart was broken and her course in life was set – she had turned to the dark side.'

'And she told you all that?' I asked.

'She didn't need to . . . *I* was the creature.'

CHAPTER 13

For a second no one spoke. Then Ruby sighed. 'So, let me get this straight, Brimstone. You were Pallidia's pet before she turned to the dark side?

'She was a good person back then,' he said with a sniff.

Ruby rolled her eyes. 'And now we've gone back in time to stop the thieving old sea captain – Septimus Silver-whatsit – from stealing you, or rather the old you, the younger you, so Pallidia won't turn bad?' She puffed out her cheeks. 'That's mad! Even if we *can* stop her, won't Pallidia's dark side just show up some other time? I mean, what if someone else cheeses her off, won't it all happen again? We can't exactly hang around in history, making sure she behaves herself.'

Brimstone boggled Ruby grumpily. 'Pallidia was on

the cusp. That's why it all went wrong. If the sea captain had pinched me a few weeks later, after the summer solstice when she'd have chosen the life of stitch witchery, then none of this would have happened!'

'Bit of a waste though,' said Ruby, tapping her teeth with her finger.

'What do you mean?' I asked.

'Well,' she said with a shrug, 'Pallidia's an exceptionally powerful witch. I can't quite picture her wasting her days sewing men's pants. How dull is that? Have you ever tried it, Tom? Nope? Well let me tell you – sewing is boring. And for Pallidia it would have been even worse. Like Lionel Messi being forced to play for Middle Spit Sands under-elevens!'

'Better to spend your time sewing suits than stealing souls,' I said firmly.

Ruby shrugged. 'S'pose so.' But I didn't think she meant it.

'How did Pallidia get you back?' I asked Brimstone.

'As I told you, another witch found me when I washed up on a beach further down the coast. She was a snitch witch . . .'

'A sneaky spy,' said Ruby with a frown. 'They're not

very powerful,' she added for my benefit, 'but they're very sly. They have clammy hands and small eyes. Looking at one always gives me the creeps.'

'Anyway,' continued Brimstone, 'Pallidia heard the snitch witch had found me and she stole me back. But by then the damage was done. Pallidia had changed. She'd turned to the dark side and didn't want me to be her pet any more; she wanted me to be her familiar, to help her steal souls. She enchanted me, so I could speak, and taught me enough magic to be useful. But she knew my heart wasn't in it . . .'

I looked back at the lighthouse. It looked so strong and dependable, not the evil den of a soul-stealing maniac. Then I remembered we'd gone back in time and it wasn't . . . yet . . .

'Come on,' I said with a sudden burst of energy. 'We've got to try and stop Pallidia!'

I jumped off the blanket, ready to swim ashore. But as I did, I stumbled, and my feet sank into sand. We'd reached the shallows and the water barely came up to my knees. I shivered as my shoes filled with sea water.

'What about the blanket?' asked Ruby.

I picked up its control panel and half a bucket of

water poured out. 'It doesn't look like we'll be going back to the future any time soon. Not until this thing dries out.'

As I shook away the last of the water, a long silver feather fell out the back of the control panel. It looked just like the one I'd seen Pallidia remove from it when we'd first arrived at the Lighthouse of Souls.

'The summoner,' said Brimstone knowledgably. 'The spare, I think. Every blanket has two, just in case one gets lost. They're not supposed to be kept with the blanket, but Pallidia must have forgotten to take it out. Keep it safe, Tom.'

'Why? What does it do?'

'It summons the blanket.'

I was just about to ask how it worked when I felt a stone whizz past my ear. And then another one thwacked into my shin. 'Ouch!'

'What circus have you run away from?'

A group of mucky looking boys were pointing at us. I looked down at our clothes – jeans, T-shirts, trainers – normal 21st-century clothes, but totally different to what they were wearing.

'Er . . . hi . . .' I grinned, wading towards them.

'Where did you come from?' A snub-nosed boy in an oversized cap demanded. 'The moon?'

'Ha,' I laughed, trying not to pick a fight. But I could see other people on the beach staring at us too. We stood out like pirates at a princess party. A few of the grown-ups were nudging each other and whispering. I tried not to meet their eyes as I hauled the Snooze Cruiser on to the shingle.

'What's that?' said another boy, pointing at the blanket.

'And what's in your hair?' said a third, touching my head. As he did there was a sudden burst of static and he drew his hand away like he'd been burned. He poked me hard in the chest. 'Freak!'

I gritted my teeth. I hate fighting. I'm not any good at it. But just then a streak of red hurtled past me and threw itself on the lad. And suddenly there was an ugly scuffle of legs, arms and elbows.

'Ruby,' I yelled. 'Stop!'

'It's a bloomin' girl!' I heard one of the boys shout, as Ruby gave him a thump.

Then the others piled in. I groaned. We were never going to blend in now. 'Ger-off her,' I shouted, trying to pull a couple of the smaller lads away. But one of them turned and gave me a smack on the arm. And suddenly I was throwing punches too, just as a whistle blew from across the beach.

'Bobbies!' one of the kids yelped and the gang scattered like pigeons. The whistle blew again and I hauled Ruby to her feet, ready to scarper. But it wasn't the police, it was a strange group of people who'd appeared at the far end of the shingle, banging drums and blowing whistles, attracting a small crowd around them.

'Acrobats,' beamed Ruby.

Two young men were cartwheeling across the sand, followed by a third, who was juggling green bottles. Behind them was a fair-haired girl in a purple frock, balancing on top of a white pony . . .

'Come and see the Great Leap-a-leenies,' she was shouting. 'Direct from the Grand Pier at Sunny Bay . . .'

Ruby's face lit up, and she trotted towards them like a fly spotting a sticky bun.

'Wait,' I called. 'What about the Snooze Cruiser?'

But Ruby wasn't listening. Typical! So I dragged the blanket over to some rocks where Brimstone was waiting and laid it out to dry. I just hoped none of the crazy history people would come and nab it.

'Tom! Over here!' Ruby was right up close to the acrobats now, waving at me to follow. Brimstone climbed reluctantly on to my arm and we headed over, my wet shoes squelching on the shingle.

As we got closer, I saw there were more performers – a fire-eater, a knife thrower, and several men walking on their hands. They were all brightly costumed so they stood out like pimples among the dark-suited and heavy-frocked holidaymakers who watched them.

'Join in, Ruby,' I whispered, as an idea suddenly came to me. 'At the back, I mean.'

'What?'

'People won't notice how odd we look if they think we're with the circus. Come on!'

We weaved through the crowd and found places at the back of the queue, just behind an old man and his performing poodles.

'Wave,' I hissed to Ruby. 'And smile.'

'What about me?' whispered Brimstone.

'Just try to look like you're our exotic performing pet!' I grinned.

For the next forty minutes, we trooped around town, waving and smiling and trying to look like we belonged, all the while keeping an eye open for Pallidia's clothes shop. According to the clock near the front of town, it was a little after 1pm now, but as Brimstone had no idea when he'd been stolen, we didn't know how much time we had to prevent it from happening.

As we passed a café, my tummy rumbled. Heck, I hadn't eaten for a hundred years!

'That's my mate Davie's café,' said Ruby. 'Or it will be one day. They do amazing ice-cream sundaes.'

We peered in through the windows as we passed by, but it looked dark and bare and full of long-skirted grannies with grumpy faces sipping tea. I definitely couldn't see any ice cream.

'It's all so weird,' said Ruby. 'I mean the town *looks* like Middle Spit Sands. But it's not. The shops are all wrong.'

And then I spotted something that made my heart stop. 'Ruby! Look!'

A tall, black-clad figure wearing a long dress and bonnet was striding along the pavement carrying a large basket. The face was young. And slightly sulky looking. But there was no mistaking who it was . . .

'Pallidia,' breathed Ruby.

It was true. Younger and softer-looking, and without the dark glasses, of course. But it was definitely her.

We watched as she stalked past us and disappeared down the street.

'That was freaky,' said Ruby. 'I kept waiting for her to spot us and go crazy.'

'She must be out doing her deliveries,' whispered Brimstone, 'which means I'm in the shop and about to be stolen. Quick! We've got to stop the sea captain!'

The performers were leaving town now, following a path that led up towards the cliff tops, where we could see a large tent had been erected. As the crowds began to drift away, we did too. Time was running out. We had to find the shop. And fast!

CHAPTER 14

We searched every corner of the small town. We went past the switchback railway, past the butcher's shop, a fishmonger's, several souvenir stalls and an old seaside pub where sailors were singing heartily inside. And then suddenly we found it, tucked up a back street, squashed between an apothecary and a pipe shop.

Black's the Tailors was a small dark shop with a bay window and red velvet drapes. We were just about to stick our noses against the glass to peer inside when the door opened and a smart man in a black coat and top hat stalked out.

Brimstone quivered on my shoulder. 'There, that's him,' he hissed. 'That's Septimus Silverback!'

'Are you sure?' Ruby frowned. 'Only, I think he looks familiar.'

The man was younger than I'd expected, clean shaven with slightly podgy cheeks. He didn't look like a sea captain. Ruby was right, he actually looked like someone I knew. But as he brushed past us, I noticed he was clutching a large box to his chest.

'I'm in there,' wailed Brimstone. 'I'm sure of it. He's got my younger self trapped inside! We're too late!'

'No, we're not,' Ruby muttered. Head down, arms pumping air, she ran after the man. He was moving fast, as though he had a ship to catch (which he did!), but Ruby was super-speedy. As Brimstone and I reached the corner of the street, she was right behind him. And then suddenly she attacked.

'Blimey!' I gasped.

Ruby hurled herself at the man's legs, like a rugby player making a tackle. The sea captain dropped hard, cracking his head on the pavement. The box flew into the air and I managed to dive forward and catch it.

For a second everyone on the street stopped and stared. And then suddenly there was pandemonium. People surged forward to help the man, who now lay lifeless on the pavement.

'Call a doctor!' someone shouted.

'He's dead!' yelled another.

'Police!' screamed a third.

Ruby, meanwhile, slipped through their legs and appeared by my side, dusting down her jeans.

'Quick,' she said. 'Open the box!'

I was just about to when Brimstone gave a squeal. 'Wait!' he said nervously. 'Do you think it's all right for me to meet myself?'

'What?'

'I mean, won't something awful happen if I come face to face with an earlier version of myself?'

'He's got a point,' said Ruby seriously. 'There must be rules about this sort of thing . . .'

'You're both nuts,' I said, pulling open the box. As I did, we all got a shock. Ruby groaned. And Brimstone let out a moan. 'I'm not there!' he said incredulously.

He wasn't. The only thing inside the box was a hat – a top hat, a brand-new top hat, black and shiny. I picked it up and turned it over. Inside was a set of initials.

'W.S.C.' I read.

Then, like a claxon going off, Ruby gave a shriek. 'Oh, Lord, I've killed Winston Churchill!'

'What?'

'I *knew* I recognised him,' she groaned, pointing to the figure, still lying sprawled on the pavement. 'It's Winston Churchill. You know – the cigar-smoking bloke who wins World War II for us! W.S.C. – those are his initials – Winston Spencer Churchill. It's him – the younger him, before he becomes prime minister.'

'Rubbish! What would Winston Churchill be doing in Middle Spit Sands in 1912? That's mad!'

'No, it's not.' Ruby folded her arms and made a cross face. 'We studied him at school. I know loads about him. And I know for a fact that he liked to take seaside holidays near here to do painting and stuff. And he liked wearing hats, too. So it's not mad at all.

I looked at the man. Could she possibly be right?

'I've killed Winston Churchill,' wailed Ruby. 'I've changed the course of history. It's a disaster!'

'Maybe you haven't,' I murmured.

An old woman with a red shawl was pushing her way through the crowd . . .

'Let me get by,' she growled. 'I've got smelling salts to revive the gentleman.' Her voice was surprisingly deep. It reminded me of Bladderwart's – the stench witch from Dad's shop.

She bent down, pulled a small glass bottle from her basket and wafted it under the man's nose. For a few seconds nothing happened. Then suddenly he sneezed and his eyes began to twitch and blink. And then he sat up, rubbing his head, looking dazed.

'He's alive!' squealed Ruby.

Suddenly all eyes turned on us and then a voice shouted, 'That's her – the girl who did him in! I saw her do it! And look – the boy's got the gentleman's box!'

'Thieves!' someone shouted. And then rough arms were grabbing us.

'Oi!' I yelled as a stocky man in a stinky suit grasped my T-shirt.

'Gotcha,' he snapped. Then he grabbed Ruby too. And Brimstone vanished.

'Let me go!' shouted Ruby, trying to kick him.

'Thieves,' said Mr Stinky. 'You tried to rob that man!'

'Oh, I don't think they did,' said the old woman, stepping towards us. She looked up at the brown-suited man, her small eyes twinkling. Then suddenly she coughed in his face and instantly his expression changed, as though he'd been hypnotised. His frown evaporated and he let us go.

'The gentleman must have dropped his box,' said the old woman to the crowd. 'These children were trying to return it, weren't you, my dears?'

I nodded. 'Er . . . yes, that's right . . .'

The crowd didn't look convinced and I heard a few mutterings of 'Gypsies' and 'Thieves'.

'Let's go,' I whispered to Ruby. 'Thanks very much,' I added to the woman. But as I turned to leave, she grabbed my arm, her hands unmistakably clammy. And then I noticed how narrow her green eyes were. And I gulped.

'Snitch witch!' said Brimstone's voice, inside my head.

I jumped. He'd crawled in there to hide again. I gritted my teeth. I wished he wouldn't do that. It was like having someone rummaging through my brain.

'You're very welcome . . .' said the woman. 'Tom . . . and Ruby, isn't it?'

I froze. How did she know our names?

'Nice children,' she said, reaching out as if to pat Ruby's head. Too late I spotted the blade in her wrinkled fist. And in a blink she'd sliced an inch off one of Ruby's plaits.

'Oi!' yelped Ruby, jumping back.

But the woman was already moving away. 'Such a pretty colour,' she said in a singsong sort of a growl. Then she turned and vanished into the crowd.

'What was that all about?' I asked.

Ruby fingered the sawn-off end of her hair. 'Not sure, but I think it's bad. Witches use hair to make charms . . .'

'How did she know our names?'

But before she could answer, I noticed that the injured man was now attempting to stagger to his feet. Ruby stepped forward with his hat box.

'Excuse me, sir, you . . . er . . . dropped this.'

The man took the box, his face still dazed and confused-looking.

'And, er . . . Mr Churchill,' said Ruby, her face turning red. 'I just wanted to tell you not to give up in World War II – things go really bad at first and you might think about throwing in the towel, but don't, because you win in the end, okay?'

'Shut up, Rubes,' I tugged her away. 'Come on! We need to catch the real sea captain.'

CHAPTER 15

'I can't believe you did that,' said Ruby crossly. 'I was going to ask for his autograph!'

'Yeah, like that would have helped our situation.'

Ruby stuck out her tongue.

'And anyway,' I added, 'it probably wasn't even him. Maybe he just had the same initials. He was probably William Slimy Cockle-head, or something . . .'

'It *was* him,' she said sulkily. 'I know it was.'

'What does it matter?' came a small voice from my shoulder. Brimstone had morphed back again.

I turned my head and gave him a stern look. 'Will you please stop using my head as a den!'

'Why?' snapped Ruby. 'There's obviously plenty of space in there!'

For a second we glared at each other, then Brimstone

coughed. 'Can we please get back to the shop before the real thief turns up!'

We walked the rest of the way in silence. But as we turned into the backstreet where we'd found Pallidia's shop, a figure dodged out of the shadows and ran past us, disappearing before we could blink.

'That was him!' squawked Brimstone. 'The real sea captain! I saw the box! Quick!'

We gave chase, but as we raced back along the main street the figure was nowhere in sight.

'Over there!' I yelled. I'd spotted him again, a good distance away. He cast a furtive glance behind, then dashed towards a horse and carriage, which was waiting at the far end of the street.

'Stop!' I yelled.

Heads turned. People pointed. But the man didn't stop, and by the time we reached the end of the street, red-faced and puffed out, the carriage was already heading round the bend, galloping out of town.

'Pants,' I groaned.

'We can still catch him!' cried Ruby. 'Come on – we'll take the short cut up to the cliffs through the big field. Then we'll cut him off on the other side.'

We set off once more, dodging pipe-smoking gentlemen and parasol-pointing ladies, ignoring the overdressed kids who pointed at our clothes and laughed. We were on the path the circus performers had taken earlier, which rose steeply behind the town, and as I glanced back towards the beach, I realised the tide was coming in. I just hoped the Snooze Cruiser wouldn't get washed out to sea or we'd be stuck here for ever.

'Quick! Through the gate!' yelled Ruby.

Ahead of us I could see the circus tent, and in front of it were dozens of performers obviously getting ready for the afternoon show.

'Hey!' called a blonde-haired girl as we hurried past. 'If you're looking for Electra, she's in the tent with the snakes . . .'

I frowned. Electra? Who was she?

The girl smiled at me and waved, and I realised she was one of the acrobats from the parade.

'Gosh,' she said, peering at Brimstone, who was still glued to my shoulder. 'Is that Electra's new creature? How exciting! Does it breathe fire?'

Brimstone boggled her nervously.

'Come on, Tom,' yelled Ruby. 'Quick, or we'll miss the coach!'

'Hey,' called the girl. 'You're going the wrong way – I told you, Electra's in the tent!'

But just then there was the sound of excited yapping, and a dozen pink-rinsed poodles raced out of a nearby caravan and surrounded us.

Brimstone instantly morphed, but I was ready for him. I stuck my fingers in my ears, so he couldn't get inside my head, and instead of a mind maggot he changed into a butterfly and flapped around my head.

'Gerr-off!' yelled Ruby, trying to shake away several poodles, who were fussing around her legs. 'Dogs always do this to me – my bones must smell good or something.'

In the distance I could hear the sound of horses' hooves . . .

'Quick, Tom,' Ruby yelled. 'Try and stop the coach!'

I dodged past the dogs and raced across the field. The road was in sight now. And so was the carriage, thundering towards me. I could beat it. I knew I could (even with super-squelchy trainers and soggy jeans). I ran so fast I felt my heart was about to explode out of my chest. And I would have made it too, if the knife hadn't appeared . . .

Just as I was within a whisker of reaching the road, a silver blade whistled past my ears, hitting the fence a few feet in front of me, closely followed by another. I pulled up fast as a third blade hurtled overhead.

'Oi! You there!'

In the seconds that I lost looking to see who was throwing knives, the carriage sailed past on the road in front of me, and Brimstone's younger self was gone for ever.

'Are you the boy they sent up from the village?' boomed the voice. It actually sounded quite friendly. It came from the knife thrower I'd seen in the parade. Big and barrel-chested, with leather trousers and a red silk shirt, he stalked over to collect his blades from the fence. 'My assistant's got the fever,' he added cheerfully. 'Probably won't last the night. So I need you for the show.'

He gave me a hearty shove back towards camp. 'Hurry up and get into your costume, the two o'clock show starts in ten minutes and trust me, if you're going to be hit by a knife, far better to be dressed in a red shirt! Much less mess!' As he laughed his large ginger moustache wriggled like a fat worm. Then he pointed to a battered and broken-looking gypsy caravan that was stuck in a mud slick on the edge of the field. 'The costume's in there,' he said giving me another shove.

'Get changed while I fetch the rest of the knives. And be quick about it!'

I was so shocked I did as I was told. I stumbled towards the caravan, and on my way I passed another caravan with 'Electra the Snake Queen' painted on the side. Something small and red darted out from behind it. It was Ruby.

'Tom! What are you doing?' she hissed.

'Er . . . well . . .'

'Did you stop the coach?' she interrupted. 'And get 1912 Brimstone back?'

I shook my head. 'I got nobbled by the knife thrower. He thinks I'm his new assistant.'

'Good grief! Can't you stay out of trouble for two minutes?'

Ha, she could talk!

'Come on,' Ruby frowned. 'We've got to get out of here. Maybe we can still stop young Pallidia from going ballistic. Try to get her parents to lock her in the shop or something . . .'

I followed Ruby back through the camp, hoping the knife thrower wouldn't spot me, then suddenly I stopped. 'Where's Brimstone?' I asked.

Ruby cocked her head to one side. 'He was with you.'

'He was, but he changed into a butterfly when the dogs appeared. I haven't seen him since.'

'Great,' said Ruby through gritted teeth. 'We'll have to find him before we can go after Pallidia.' She looked around. 'You go that way, I'll try down the other side, there are loads more caravans there. And stay away from the knife man, okay!'

But the audience for the afternoon show was already entering the tent, and it was hard to see anything amongst the old-fashioned frocks and handlebar moustaches. Butterfly Brimstone could be anywhere!

And then things went from bad to terrible. I felt a large podgy hand on my shoulder. 'There you are! Why haven't you changed?' It was the knife thrower and he didn't look happy. 'Oh well, you'll just have to do.' He threw a mock punch at my arm. 'Lucky for you my aim's always good in the afternoon.' Then he dragged me into the tent.

I tried to protest, but as we stepped inside the smell nearly floored me – the place stank! It was a hot afternoon anyway, but the smell from the sweaty bodies squished together was overpowering.

The knife thrower handed me a basket of dirty-looking blades. 'There you go, lad. Now smile and wave!' And suddenly we were in the ring, walking behind two clowns. 'Wave,' he said, giving me a thump on the back.

So I did, until I spotted someone waving back. It was Ruby, standing near the exit making an exasperated face. I was just about to leg it over to her when I felt the knife thrower's hand on my shoulder again.

'Over here, lad,' he said. 'We need to wait a moment while the other performers greet the audience, then we'll be the first act on!' He pulled me out of the ring over towards a pile of hay bales, where the acrobats' ponies were waiting.

'Hello again,' said a kind voice. And I recognised the blonde acrobat girl who I'd seen earlier. 'I see Old Harry's got you helping out.' Then she bent closer and whispered in my ear, 'Best not to work in the evening show – he likes a drink after this and his aim won't be so good later on!' She winked at me. 'My name's Lena, by the way. What's yours?'

'Tom,' I said. 'Though I'm not supposed to be here. It's all been a big mistake!'

But Lena didn't hear me because just then a band marched noisily past us. Lena gave me a wave and then went to join the rest of the acrobats who were standing further back.

'Psssst!' I glanced round and spotted Ruby peering at me from under the edge of the tent. 'Come on, Tom,' she hissed. 'Let's go!' And I was about to join her when the knife thrower grabbed my arm again. The band had stopped playing now and there was a loud drum roll. Then a voice form the ring shouted: 'Introducing Haraldo Steel, the knight of a thousand knives!'

'We're on,' he grinned. The spotlight found us, and I was dragged into the ring. It wasn't until I saw the men rolling in a huge circular archery target that it dawned on me what was about to happen . . .

'Er . . . wait a minute . . .' I stammered, as the knife thrower led me towards the target, all the time waving and smiling at the audience. 'I'm not really supposed to be here . . . there's been a bit of a mix up . . .'

'You stand like this, okay?' The knife thrower said, taking the basket of knives from me and pushing me in front of the target, with my hands by my side. 'Don't move.' He winked. 'Or you'll get hit!' Then he turned and began pacing his way up to the other end of the ring, where he placed the basket of knives. I should have made a run for it then, but I hesitated for a second, momentarily carried away by the spotlight and the hundreds of excited faces watching me. Then I spotted the knife thrower picking up a fistful of blades and my belly lurched. And suddenly I couldn't run, because the first blade was already whizzing towards me.

'Aaargh!' I shouted. Or I would have done if my throat hadn't spontaneously dried up like the Sahara desert. Instead, I shut my eyes and did the 'La La La' thing my gran does whenever a pigeon comes near her. (She's terrified of pigeons and whenever one approaches, she closes her eyes and sings 'La La La' really loudly to pretend its not there!)

'La La La!' I sang, as I felt the target quiver behind me as three more knives thwacked into it. They were in a line down my side – a smidge away from skewering me like a shish-kebab!

'La La La!' I sang even louder as three more knives thwacked down my other side. Then one hit the target a hair's breadth above my head and the audience cheered and clapped and whooped at the danger of it! Then suddenly there were no more thwacks, and I cautiously opened one eye. Maybe it was over?

But the knife thrower was rummaging in his basket, and then my heart stopped as I saw what he was looking for. Machetes – the weapons of choice for mad axemen! But there was worse to come. The knife thrower had pulled out a black scarf and was wrapping it round his eyes. I gasped. He was about to play 'pin the tail on the donkey' with a machete and my head!

I'd had enough now. I didn't care that the audience loved me. I was off. Only I wasn't, because there was a slight problem with my trousers. They were pinned to the target by the knives. Maybe that had been the knife thrower's plan, to stop me escaping. I tugged at the fabric, but it was held fast. Then the drum roll began again, and the blindfolded knife thrower prepared to attack. But just as he lifted the first axe, there was a sudden scuffle down his end, and the knife thrower disappeared. I ripped my trousers free from one side of the target and was starting on the second when the knife thrower returned – only it wasn't him! I heard a horribly familiar cackle and a dark figure with long back hair appeared in his place. My eyes popped like corn.

'Pallidia!' I gasped.

CHAPTER 16

It was her. Not the young Pallidia who we were trying to save from herself. This was the scary old witch from the lighthouse! There she was, standing with an armful of machetes, all aimed at me. Behind her I could see a figure sprawled on the tent floor – the knife thrower I presumed. Not that the audience noticed. They obviously thought it was all part of the act.

I desperately tried to free the other half of my trousers to escape. But it was too late. With another stomach-churning cackle she threw the first axe. I shut my eyes, waiting for the blade to hit me. It did. But just the top of my hair! Strands fluttered down on to my face like confetti.

'Ha!' I heard Pallidia cackle, and then she threw the next axe. This time I didn't hesitate. I leapt out of the way, ripping my jeans as I moved. I glanced back to see the axe hit the target precisely where my nose had just been. It feels weird to know you've just missed certain death. And for a second I stood there, gawping at the place where I would have died . . .

'Quick, Tom,' I heard Ruby shout. 'This way!'

I stopped gawping and tried to work out where she was. But under the spotlight I was suddenly disorientated. I could see nothing but strange faces, all peering back at me. Then I saw Pallidia lining up another axe to throw at me, and I dived for my life – straight into the audience. There were screams and squeals as I floundered over legs and knees, squishing faces with my hands, and treading on toes.

The lights had gone up now and I could see Lena and the other acrobats standing over the knife thrower, shock and horror on their faces. The crowd began to shuffle and whisper, and then I heard someone shout for a doctor. Even more worryingly, Pallidia had vanished.

'Tom! Over here!' Ruby was waiting at the end of the row of seats that I was struggling along. I stepped across an extra-large man, using his flat cap for a hand hold, and finally reached her.

'Pallidia's here!' I gasped.

Ruby clutched my arm. 'I know, I know. I saw her too.' She dragged me towards the door of the tent. 'And I know exactly how she found us. The snitch witch used my hair!'

'What? I don't understand,' I said, tripping over a few poodles that were waiting near the door.

'It's simple. Pallidia must have known we'd used her blanket to go back in time, and so she sent a message to snitch witches across the centuries to look out for us. The woman who took my hair must have burned it in a spell to show Pallidia where to find us – like a bookmark in time – or a crease on a page . . .'

'That's mad!'

'No madder than me nearly killing Winston Churchill,' twinkled Ruby.

I couldn't argue with that.

As we raced out of the tent, back into the sunshine of the afternoon, I breathed in deeply. The air smelled good. And despite everything I felt a surge of hope. We could do this. Even with the worst witch in the world wanting to throw axes at me, we could still stop young Pallidia from turning bad. We had to.

But then Ruby suddenly stopped in her tracks. 'Aren't you forgetting something? We still haven't found Brimstone!'

'Perhaps I can help you with that problem!'

We spun round. It was Pallidia – bad, axe-throwing Pallidia. (Though, thankfully still wearing her specs, so obviously not about to steal our souls . . . yet.)

'Is this what you're looking for?' She tapped her chest, and I noticed a small brooch there. Except it wasn't a brooch . . . it was Brimstone. He wiggled one butterfly wing pathetically. The other had been cruelly skewered by the pin that fixed him to Pallidia's shirt. 'Punishment for his treachery,' said the witch, flicking his free wing cruelly with a fingernail.

I bit my lip. I felt like crying. But boys don't cry. And certainly not in front of girls – witchy or otherwise.

Pallidia smiled at us. She looked like a cat that had caught three mice by the tails. 'That was a clever trick to run away into the past,' she said, her voice a gentle purr. 'I admire your spirit . . . I could use creatures like you . . .' Then her face turned dark again. 'But I won't let you change my fate . . .'

'Oh, we weren't planning anything like that,' squeaked Ruby, her fib turning her face red like her hair. 'It was all a big mistake. We didn't mean to come back in time. Tom was just trying to get us home, and his finger slipped . . .'

'Great,' I muttered. 'Blame it on me.'

'But he's a Kirk,' spat Pallidia. 'Kirks don't make mistakes!'

'Oh, this one does,' said Ruby with a sigh. 'He's not like his dad at all.'

'Well if he's so useless he won't be missed,' said Pallidia. 'Neither of you will. Because you won't be going back.'

'What?'

Pallidia twirled around and I saw something familiar rolled up and strung across her back.

'The Snooze Cruiser!' I yelped.

'How else did you think I got here?' she snapped. 'I phoned your father, Tom, and I asked him how to recall a stolen Snooze Cruiser from the past. He was so helpful . . . he reminded me that I only had to summon the blanket with the Pegasus feather, and it would come back, even from another century . . .'

At the mention of my dad, I felt a lump of sadness in my throat. If only he was here now, he could fix things.

'Of course I didn't tell him about you,' grinned the witch. 'Although he sounded quite frantic with worry,' she smirked. 'Said his son was missing . . .'

'Traitor,' snapped Ruby, scowling at the blanket. 'How could you!'

'The Snooze Cruiser's in a terrible mess,' said Pallidia. 'But I'll forgive you, because you must be so disappointed your little plan hasn't worked. You can deny it all you like, but I know exactly what you're up to. And you can't stop me becoming me. My future is set. But look on the bright side. I've decided to let you live. Here, in 1912. Though without parents it'll probably be the poor house for both of you . . . or perhaps you could join the circus!' I gritted my teeth. 'And who knows,' she smirked, 'perhaps you'll live to be really old people, and you might meet your own parents again some day . . . except you'll be older than them, of course, and older than their grandparents. Ha ha ha!' she cackled in a really witchy way.

'We can still stop you,' said Ruby her small hands balling up into fists. 'If your younger self doesn't manage to sink that ship, then you'll end up sewing pants for ever!'

'No,' spat Pallidia. 'I won't sew! Never! I'll sink the ship myself if I have to!'

'You can't,' I said without thinking. 'Your young self has to do it. It's the laws of time travel. You're just a random ghost from the future doing yet another act of evil. Your young self has to do it herself, otherwise your future won't be dark and you won't exist – not like you do now . . .'

Ruby cocked her head to one side and looked at me out of the corner of her eye. 'Are you sure, Tom?' she muttered. 'That all sounds a bit complicated.'

'Yes,' I said firmly. And I knew I was right. Ruby might know a hundred and one things no one else wants to know about Winston Churchill. But I'd seen enough sci-fi films to know that a future self can't change a past self, without the whole plot going to pot.

Pallidia considered this for a moment, then suddenly her face turned upwards towards the sky. 'Ha,' she scoffed. 'I won't need to sink that ship . . . look!'

I glanced upwards and my heart sank. The sun had gone. The sky was darkening. I felt a cold wind in the air. There was a storm approaching . . .

'No,' groaned Ruby. 'Young Pallidia must have discovered that the sea captain has stolen her pet!'

'Yes,' purred Pallidia. 'My younger self is turning dark all by herself. I might as well fetch a deck chair and sit on the beach and watch things unfold . . . it's a glorious day for a sinking . . .'

As she spoke, there was a sudden crack of lightning above us, and Pallidia cackled along with it. Really, if she didn't want to be a soul stealer she could get a job as a pantomime baddie.

Ruby's shoulders slumped slightly. 'We're too late, Tom.'

I tried to think of something encouraging to say, but the shelf of plans in the back of my brain was empty.

Just then, though, there was a shout:

'There she is! That's the woman who killed Old Harry!'

A group of circus performers was standing in the tent doorway, pointing at Pallidia.

'Oh, please,' she groaned, as though they were bothersome bees after her jam sandwich. 'I only took his soul,' she muttered. 'And to be perfectly frank, it's rather lumpy and uncomfortable . . .'

As she spoke, she pulled open the elastic on her cuff, and a brown smudgy gas escaped from within. It levitated for a few seconds in front of us, blinking and winking, its large moustache wriggling . . .

'The knife-thrower's soul,' I breathed. Then the wind blew him back towards the tent.

'If he hurries, his corpse won't be cold,' cackled Pallidia. 'And he may even live to throw another knife!'

'Witch!' shouted one of the clowns. 'Did you see what she just did?'

'She's no witch,' said Lena, who had joined the group. 'She's a murdering bully!'

Pallidia shot her a glance. 'Watch your mouth, young woman, or you might find your tightrope snaps and you break your neck!'

Lena scowled at her defiantly, but she was pushed aside by a tall man in a smart red coat who stepped forward, his cheeks rosy and his small beady eyes glowing. 'Madam, I don't care what you are, you're amazing. Have you ever thought of a career in the circus?'

And suddenly Pallidia was surrounded by circus types asking her how she'd done the trick with the gas up her sleeve . . .

'Come on,' hissed Ruby, grabbing my arm. 'Let's go, while she's not watching . . .'

We took off towards town. But with every step I could feel Pallidia's eyes on my back. She was watching all right. And I knew she wouldn't be far behind.

CHAPTER 17

'But what about Brimstone?' I puffed, trying to keep up with Ruby, who was racing ahead like a startled antelope.

'Which one?' she yelled back.

'The old one – the one stuck to Pallidia's dress!'

But she wasn't listening. She was sniffing the air. 'Hell's teeth, Tom, something's burning!'

'The switchback railway!'

As we turned the corner, people were running towards us, their white frocks and smart suits covered in soot and mess.

'The town's ablaze,' shouted one woman, waving her parasol in the air like a flag. 'Run for your lives!'

'Drama queen,' muttered Ruby, pushing past her.

Ruby was right. The woman *was* a drama queen.

The town wasn't burning . . . not yet. But the old wooden roller coaster was on fire – great orange and yellow flames spitting out of it like fireworks. The heat was intense. A group of shopkeepers and fisher folk had made a chain from the seashore, passing up buckets of water to throw on it. I was about to join in when Ruby nudged me. Further along the beach was a familiar black figure pushing a rowing boat into the water.

'Pallidia!' yelled Ruby. 'Young Pallidia! Come on, Tom! We can still stop her from reaching the lighthouse.'

It was raining now and the wind had picked up. As we moved away from the flames, the cold struck me like a stone. I shivered. I suddenly felt tired and thirsty and weary to the bone.

'Come on, Tom!' said Ruby, grabbing my hand. 'We have to stop Pallidia!'

But she was already in the water, rowing hard against the waves.

'If only we had the blanket!' Ruby wailed.

And then I remembered the summoner – the feather that had fallen out of the back of the control panel.

I reached into my pocket. It was still there. 'Ruby,' I breathed, pulling it out. 'Look! Brimstone said it was the spare summoner . . .'

She shrugged.

'Don't your mum and dad keep a spare key to your car anywhere, just in case they lock their own key in the car, or lose it?'

'S'pose so . . . but, Tom, we don't have the blanket here, so what good is a spare key?'

'Because this isn't a key – it's a device to call the blanket. That was how Old Pallidia recalled the blanket from the past. She used the summoner. Brimstone said there was a spare one, and this is it!'

'I still don't see how that helps us,' said Ruby impatiently. 'And look, young Pallidia's miles out now, we'll never stop her!'

I held the feather in my hand. I traced my finger down its pale silver spine. If only I knew how to use it. I tapped it on my hand, once, twice, then harder. Instantly a small puff of smoke shot out of the bottom.

Ruby's eyes widened.

I did it again, slapping it against the palm of my hand. An even bigger puff of smoke popped out.

Then I tried it once more. This time I thumped it really hard. And with a loud crack! a bullet of blue light shot out of the end, ricocheted off the shingle and shot up into the sky, where it burst open like a firework, showering us in fizzing embers.

For a while we just stood there gawping upwards, and then suddenly Ruby gave a shout. 'Look!'

A dark shadow was hurtling towards us like a missile.

'The blanket,' I screamed. 'It worked!'

We watched in wonder as the familiar shape spiralled down on to the beach, eventually stopping a few feet away, where it hovered shyly, buffeted by the rain and wind.

'Come on, Ruby!' As I pulled myself on board, the blanket felt damp to touch and still smelled faintly of Bladderwart's pipe smoke, but there was something reassuringly friendly and comforting about it too. Ruby climbed up beside me.

'Sorry about the "traitor" thing,' she muttered into the blanket. It wriggled slightly, as though it understood.

'What about the control panel?' asked Ruby.

The words were barely out of her mouth before the thing fell out of the air on to my lap.

'Thanks,' I grinned. This time I didn't try to think how to fly the blanket, I just placed my hands on the controls, where they moved instinctively beneath my fingers. And suddenly we were off, flying low above the sand, the blanket too full of sand and water and rain to fly much higher. The wind was buffeting us too. But we didn't notice. We didn't even attempt to find the air shield. We just sat low in the centre of the blanket, our faces wet with the rain that lashed us as we stared out towards the white dot on the horizon . . . towards the Lighthouse of Souls, where our fate would decide Pallidia's future.

CHAPTER 18

As we flew above the water, we suddenly saw them. Dark shadows rippling menacingly in the sea below.

'What are they?' I yelled above the noise of the wind and rain.

As I spoke, a large head emerged from the water. The face was long, the nostrils were flared, and for a moment I thought it might be some sort of sea monster . . .

'Hell's teeth, Tom,' gasped Ruby. 'I think it's a kelpie!'

'A what?'

'A water horse!'

'Like a seahorse, you mean?'

'No, something way worse than that. Kelpies are bad. Really bad. They're magical sea creatures that drown humans.'

'Whoa!' I shouted, as one of the creatures suddenly

reared up out of the sea, its heavy hooves pounding
the froth of the waves. It reached its long neck towards
us, trying to nip the blanket with its large green teeth.
Instinctively, I pulled back the lever my right hand was
resting on, and the blanket lifted slightly, just enough
to escape the kelpie's jaws. But then another one reared
up, even larger than the last . . .

I dodged the control right, and the blanket flipped
up, only just missing the creature this time.

'It's her!' yelled Ruby, looking back over her
shoulder towards the beach. 'Old Pallidia's there, I can
see her – she's calling up the kelpies!'

But I didn't have time to look back; I was too busy trying to keep the blanket out of the creatures' reach. But we were struggling. Weighed down with sand and water and the lashing rain and strong winds, the blanket was slowing and sinking ever lower. Instead of rising out of the creatures' way, I was having to dodge round them instead.

'Ruby,' I called. 'We need to make the blanket lighter!'

'What?'

'It's too heavy – we're going down!'

Just then, one of the kelpies' mouths grabbed a corner of the blanket and began tugging us towards the sea. I kicked out with my leg, hitting the creature between the eyes. It shrieked and whined and let go briefly. And the blanket shot back up.

'Quick, Ruby! We need to lose some stuff off the blanket.'

'But there's only us on it!' screamed Ruby. 'And I don't fancy taking a dive in the sea, thanks very much!'

'Look in the pockets!' I yelled.

'There aren't any!'

'You can't see them, but they're there. You just have

to believe that they're there, and then you'll feel them. Quick, start chucking stuff out . . .'

But just then a snorting head appeared next to Ruby, a spitting kelpie with snapping jaws. Ruby threw a punch, smacking the creature hard on the nose. The whites of its eyes rolled back wildly into its head, green slime poured from its nose. Then it shrank back into the water.

'Come on, Ruby, do something!'

'Okay, okay,' she shouted, stuffing her hands into invisible pockets all around the edges of the blanket. 'But there's nothing here,' she wailed.

'Keep looking!'

And then . . .

'I've got something,' she shouted triumphantly, and she hauled out a large book. Without looking to see what it was she thwacked it into the face of a screaming kelpie, who had suddenly loomed up behind us. Half a dozen books followed. Each one went over the side. Then there were a few boxes . . . one that looked like it contained tools. I grimaced. I hoped we wouldn't need them later, then I remembered I couldn't fix anything anyway!

Ruby went on pulling out stuff, like a magician with a top hat – pillows, blankets, an old lamp. A hair dryer, several maps, boxes, a flask, three mugs, a set of spoons and a heavy coat that looked like it was made of yeti fur. It smelled like it too . . .

'It's working!' I yelled. 'We're rising, Ruby!' And we were. The more stuff she threw over the side, the higher we went.

Four stools, a camping stove, sixteen, no . . . seventeen tins of sardines. A sack of garden gnomes, a crate of matches, a tub labelled toad tongues, and three pickled eyeballs in a huge glass jar. A beach towel. A wooden peg leg. A plastic lilo. A sack of scarves. A tub of rubber ducks and a bucket of soap. As each thing splashed into the sea we went higher and higher until we were out of reach of the kelpies. I watched them disappear, one by one diving back into the water. Then Ruby stopped throwing stuff and collapsed by my side.

'We did it,' she grinned. But her smile vanished as a sudden lightning bolt cracked above her head. Its silvery fingers hit the blanket and I smelled burning.

'Watch it!' I shouted.

The lightning had scorched the blanket in the shape of a snake. As we watched, the scorch mark turned green then began to form into a real snake, just like the one on Pallidia's cheek.

Ruby leapt away from it, making the blanket wobble wildly. But I was frozen to the spot while the creature eyeballed me, its tongue spitting out, tasting the air. Then its tail began to rattle . . .

'I saw a telly programme about rattlesnakes,' I whispered.

'How do you kill 'em?' squeaked Ruby.

'You can't . . . they're a protected species. You just need to back away from them.'

Ruby peered into the inky sea below. 'I don't think that's going to work, Tom.'

For a second I wondered if I should just make a lunge for it, get it round the neck, like they do on telly. The creature swayed threateningly in front of me, as though it had read my mind.

'Wait, Tom,' said Ruby, suddenly sounding more confident. 'I've got an idea . . .'

'What?'

'You know I told you I want to be a witch . . .'

'Yeah?'

'Well . . . I know one spell. A friendly witch taught it to me . . .'

'How to turn a snake into a spoon?' I asked hopefully.

But she didn't reply. She was wiggling her finger in little circles at the creature, as though trying to hypnotise it, all the while chanting softly to herself.

Then there was a phuff! sound, as though a damp party popper had gone off, and suddenly the blanket was covered with stuff. Cups, saucers, boxes, plates, a bag of dirty underwear that spilled open, scattering socks and pants across our feet . . . a sack of potatoes, a deck chair, a cage of little white mice that squeaked and scratched, five hats, several books, a spade, a food mixer and a small sack of unopened letters that looked like unpaid bills.

'I did it,' said Ruby brightly. 'I made the snake disappear!'

But just then I heard the horrible rattling noise again, and from beneath the dirty washing a green triangular head reappeared.

'What was that spell?'

Ruby's face turned red. 'It's a stock-taking spell,' she said. 'It gets all your stuff out so you can count it. A list witch taught it to me . . .'

'Great,' I said through gritted teeth. 'Really helpful, if you want to find your dirty pants!'

Ruby made a face. But just then there was a sudden gust of wind, and the blanket flipped up, flinging everything into the air. When it all bumped back down, the cage door shot open and the white mice escaped.

It was too much for the snake. Its eyes darted left, right, then it pounced for one. But the mouse was too fast. It dropped into an invisible pocket, while the snake overshot and plummeted off the blanket into the sea below.

'It worked,' screamed Ruby. 'My spell worked!'

And I suppose it had . . . sort of.

But Ruby didn't get time to enjoy her moment of glory, because I'd spotted something looming behind her . . .

'Look, Ruby – the lighthouse!'

CHAPTER 19

We were close now. Just seconds away from having to confront young Pallidia.

'That's the lighthouse keeper,' said Ruby, pointing to a rowing boat with a small figure lying in it that was being buffeted wildly by the sea. 'Pallidia must have knocked him out and put him in the boat . . .'

I pulled back on the controls and the blanket slowed even more, then we began to fall. Too fast! For a terrible moment I thought we were about to be dashed on the rocks. Then a gust of wind blew us towards the stone jetty at the front of the lighthouse, where we landed heavily. The waves were crashing around us, as though trying to smash us back into the sea. But we were running on adrenalin now. We were close. So close. We had to stop Pallidia!

We dragged the blanket along the jetty, rolled it up, then heaved open the iron door of the lighthouse. It was strange to be back inside. It looked so different now. Welcoming and friendly, with bright whitewashed walls. A hurricane lamp lit the hall. I picked it up and we began to climb the stairs, carrying the blanket between us.

'Sssh!' hissed Ruby, as my wet trainers squelched and squeaked on the stone steps. I glared at her. I couldn't help it! Then as we neared the top she leaned over and whispered, 'What's the plan?'

I shrugged. Then grinned. There never had been a plan. I thought Ruby might be cross with me. But she smiled and clasped my hand and squeezed it in a good luck sort of a way. I thought for one terrible moment she was about to kiss me too . . . but just then there was a shout from above:

'Who's there?'

The voice echoed down the stairs around us. It was young. And not particularly witchy-sounding. But there was no mistaking the owner. Pallidia Black – the angry, teenage Pallidia.

'Er . . . hello . . . my name's Ruby and this is Tom . . .'

As we turned the corner into the lamp room, where the lighthouse light was rhythmically rotating, casting its reassuring beam out to sea, there she was, looming blackly in the corner, where she'd obviously been keeping watch for the paddle steamer . . .

'What do you want?' she glared, her eyes black with hatred.

'To save your soul,' said Ruby brightly.

I groaned. I was hoping we could try and trick Pallidia with some elaborate story about our boat having capsized and how we'd rescued our mother's blanket, which we had to return to her soon or we'd be in terrible trouble . . . then when she wasn't looking, perhaps we could just shut her in a cupboard, or something!

'Save my soul?' spat young Pallidia. 'What are you talking about?'

'What you're about to do is very bad,' said Ruby. 'And if you do it, you'll regret it for ever . . .' Then she cocked her head to one side. 'Actually,' she said. 'That last bit's not true . . .'

'Ruby,' I growled, 'you're not helping things!' I stepped forward. 'Look,' I said, 'we know you're angry, but if you sink that paddle steamer you won't get Brimstone back . . . not today anyway.'

'How do you know about Brimstone?' Pallidia's face darkened. 'Are you in league with the thief?'

'No!' we both said together.

'We're children from the future,' said Ruby, as though that was a perfectly understandable concept for an Edwardian stitch witch to grasp. 'And we've come back in time to save you from yourself . . . because me and Tom have seen how you become, and to be honest, you're not the nicest witch I've ever met.'

Pallidia's eyes flashed. 'Get out of here,' she screamed. 'Before I toss you to the rocks!'

'Great,' I muttered. 'Good job, Ruby.' You see, I knew this was not the way to deal with a teenager. My cousin Betty is one. And she's truly gruesome. Even worse than a witch on the cusp. She slams doors and screams and shouts and tells everyone how much she hates them. And according to my aunt (her mum), the only way to treat a grumpy teenager is to leave them be. Like a cross crab. Wait until they've cooled off. The thing you mustn't do is poke them with a stick, which is exactly what Ruby was doing now.

'Listen, Pallidia,' she said, 'we're trying to help you. Trust me, stealing souls is not the way to get back at this sea captain.'

'Stealing souls? What are you talking about?' shrieked Pallidia. She took a step forward and raised a hand towards us as though about to nuke us with a lightning bolt.

'Hey! Look! What's that?' I shouted – pointing towards the window. I'd only meant to distract her, but unfortunately there *was* something outside. The *SS Louisa* had appeared in the distance.

'Ha!' shouted Pallidia.

'Terrific,' said Ruby, rolling her eyes at me. 'Well played, Tom.'

'At least I wasn't about to get us turned into toast,' I hissed back.

Then the lighthouse light went out. And young Pallidia gave a horrible cackle.

'The ship!' I yelled. 'Pallidia, turn the light back on, please . . . if you don't, they'll all die. Please . . . we'll get Brimstone back for you . . . somehow.'

'Leave me alone,' Pallidia hissed through the darkness. Then lightning crackled in the sky above us, momentarily lighting up the room, and I could see her outline standing looking out to sea. A fog had descended, but even so I was sure I could make out the twinkling lights of the *SS Louisa,* close now, really close. Then suddenly we heard an ear-splitting ripping sound. And moments later a warning horn sounded.

'Ha! They've hit the needles!' hissed Pallidia. And around her body a green glow appeared. 'Now to find that thief . . .'

We couldn't let her go. I had to stop her. But how? As she turned, I slipped off my soggy trainer and threw it. Hard! Unfortunately, in the darkness it missed her completely and smacked the wall instead, knocking off a great lump of plaster.

'Shame about your aim,' said Pallidia with a sneer. Then she stepped carefully over my shoe and headed for the stairs.

Ruby gave chase, trying her Winston Churchill rugby tackle again, but the witch was made of tougher stuff than the future prime minister. She turned round and slapped Ruby away, felling her with one swipe. Ruby landed heavily on the stone floor. I was about to chase after Pallidia myself, but just then another bolt of lightning lit up the room and I caught sight of something that made me stop. The dent I'd made in the wall, where the whitewash and plaster had cracked off, had revealed the outline of a single brick. Was it my imagination, or was it red coloured . . .

'Ruby,' I breathed. 'The witch brick!'

'What?' She sat up, rubbing her jaw.

'I need some light . . .' I reached for the hurricane lamp and held it closer to the brick. I traced the outline with my finger. As I did, more plaster fell off, revealing the surrounding bricks. But only one of them was red. I touched it. I pressed it. And the brick appeared to tremble slightly. 'Don't you remember what Brimstone said . . .' I whispered. 'The old lighthouse engineers were superstitious . . . so every lighthouse they built had a single brick that could bring the whole thing down, just in case it ever got into the wrong hands, into the hands of a witch.

'So?'

'So, I'm going to pull out this brick and bring down the lighthouse on young Pallidia's head. Then the passengers of the boat will escape on the lifeboats before she can get to them.'

'And you're going to get that brick out now, before she gets out of here, with your bare hands?'

'Yes!' I began to scrabble madly at the stone. Then I remembered my name badge, the one I wore in Dad's shop. It was still pinned to my front. I took it off, bent up the pin and used it to gouge out mortar. 'Help me,' I yelled. 'Come on!'

With both of us scratching the brick began to loosen. As it did the floor around us trembled slightly.

'Open the window, Ruby. When the lighthouse falls, we'll have to escape on the blanket!'

Once I'd started, the damp mortar loosened quickly and I was able to grasp the edges of the brick with both hands. Then I pulled as though my life depended on it. Which of course it did! There was a sudden sharp crack, and then the brick dislodged completely. As I pulled it out, the building shuddered slightly and there was a strange splitting sound. Plaster crumbled off the ceiling and the floor began to vibrate.

'It's cracking . . .'

I jumped on to the blanket just in time. The floor gave way and plaster and bricks began to fall around us. I pushed the controls and we shot out of the window with only seconds to spare. As I glanced back, I saw the lighthouse roof crumble in on itself.

'There she is!' yelled Ruby. Down below we could see young Pallidia stalking along the stone jetty, searching for her boat. As she glanced up, stones and bricks began raining down on her. She raised a hand as if to protect herself and then clunk! a boulder smacked her hard on the head and she collapsed like a puppet with its strings cut.

Ruby bit her lip. 'I killed a witch,' she muttered. 'That's awful. I like witches, even stroppy ones.'

'I don't think she's dead,' I said, staring out to where the paddle steamer was floundering on the rocks.

'How do you know?'

'Because look who's just appeared over there!'

Ruby glanced over. And there, clinging to the neck of the largest, ugliest kelpie, was old Pallidia – old, soul-stealing, fights-dirty Pallidia!

'If young Pallidia was dead, then her old self would be too,' I said.

Ruby cocked her head at me. 'Er . . . right . . . good,' said Ruby. 'Or is it?'

I shook my head. 'Bad! Very bad! I reckon she's waiting for the lifeboats – waiting for the sea captain to come. She's about to fulfil her own destiny.'

CHAPTER 20

Suddenly she saw us. The kelpie's hooves reared up and old Pallidia waved her fist in the air, like a warrior about to lead a battle charge. Lightning shot out of her hands and thunder rolled like kettledrums around us. Then I caught sight of Brimstone, still pinned to her shirt as a butterfly.

All at once I felt angry. I couldn't help myself. 'Let him go,' I shouted. 'Set Brimstone free!'

'What?' Pallidia's face contorted. We were close to her now – a car's length apart at most. I watched as she pulled Brimstone off her shirt, ripping his wing cruelly as she did. She held him in her outstretched palm, his lifeless body twitching slightly.

'Actually, I'm bored with him,' she said. Then she closed her fist around the butterfly, crushing it to dust.

But as she did there was a sudden screech and I realised that it was coming from the witch herself. For she was no longer holding the remains of a small, timid butterfly. In its place was a writhing electric eel that burned the hand of its former mistress.

'Wow,' shouted Ruby. 'He got you!'

The witch turned her head to Ruby and shook off her black glasses. I shut my eyes. But Ruby was too slow, she glared back defiantly at Pallidia and in a heartbeat I felt Ruby's body slump forward on the blanket next to me.

'Ruby!' I yelled, reaching out for her. Then I looked up to see a small cloud of silver mist spinning through the air towards Pallidia. 'No!' I screamed, as the cloud vanished down the witch's gullet.

The blanket lurched forward without me touching it – I seemed to be driving it with my mind. I shut my eyes, my only shield against the witch's eyes. My fists balled, stretched out in front of me. The blanket seemed to go ballistic then, cannonballing towards Pallidia's kelpie at supersonic speed. My fists struck its flanks like a tank, and the creature screamed in pain.

I was screaming too. From the impact. From anger.

From frustration. Palllidia had taken the soul of my friend. And she'd pay for it. But while the kelpie was winded, Pallidia wasn't. She clung to the creature's neck, howling with anger. I kept my eyes closed, but I could feel intense heat around me as the air crackled and burned.

I opened one eye and realised that the blanket was in the middle of a fireball. The air shield had somehow popped up giving me some protection from the inferno. But not for long. The blaze was melting it. And we were falling too – down, down into the inky black of the sea.

The blanket hissed as it hit the water, extinguishing the fire. The air shield was gone and the waves were crashing around us, bouncing us into the air then back into the water again. I choked on sea water as the waves smashed into me. Then I landed with a thud against the rock. The blanket was still somehow beneath me and softened the blow, but I was winded. For a moment I just lay there, wondering how many bones I'd broken. Then another wave battered me in the face and I dragged the blanket and myself further up the rocks.

Then I thought of Ruby. I'd lost her body in the sea. I bit my lip. I wouldn't cry. Not yet. Instead I turned and looked at the ruins of the lighthouse. It stood barely two metres tall now, with piles of bricks and broken furniture littered around the bottom. The great light itself was smashed close by.

I turned my head the other way, and through the fog and rain I could still see Pallidia, mounted on her angry water horse, searching the waves for the captain's lifeboat. And then she found it – a light in the mist. The first of the *SS Louisa's* lifeboats were drifting towards her, the crew desperately trying to find their way in the dark and mist, hoping to avoid the rocks that would rip out the bottom of their boats and finish them off.

'No!' I groaned weakly. But just when it seemed totally and utterly hopeless, there was a sudden eruption of water between me and Pallidia, like the epicentre of a volcano. I wondered if I was seeing things. I rubbed my eyes, the salt on my hands making them sting slightly, then I looked again and I realised it wasn't a volcano, it was an animal; a green-coloured whale, the size of six buses, gliding silkily beneath the surface, silver water spurting from its blow hole.

'Brimstone!' I gasped. Instinctively, I knew it was him. The whale submerged again, like a secret submarine, and then silently moved towards Pallidia. For all her super-witch sensors, she didn't spot him coming. She was too busy peering into the gloom, waiting for her chance to kill the sea captain.

Then through the fog I spotted a light flashing. The lifeboat was coming. Pallidia seemed to grow larger at the sight of it. Her kelpie reared up, its hooves pounding the crashing waves as she prepared to strike. And that's when Brimstone took her. He loomed up behind her, a true monster of the deep, and in one silent swallow he seized her in his jaws and she was gone for ever.

'Ha!' I said out loud in my most Pallidia sounding voice.

'Tom?'

I turned round, and gazed stupidly into the face of Ruby, who was sitting on the rocks by my side, shaking seaweed out of her silvery red hair.

'Why are you staring at me like that,' she snapped. 'You look like a dead goldfish.'

'I thought you were dead!'

'What?'

'Pallidia took your soul . . .'

Ruby cocked her head to one side. 'Really? You mean I've been stuck inside the belly of that witch?'

I made a face, trying to imagine the horror of being lost in Pallidia's intestine.

'Cool,' said Ruby. 'Do you think any of her magic will have rubbed off on me?'

'Oi!' A bedraggled figure was waving at us from the base of the lighthouse. Young Pallidia had emerged from under a pile of stones. She was covered in dust and dirt. But she still looked as cross as a bag of crabs.

'Where is he?' she shrieked. 'I'll get that sea captain!' And there was an ominous rumble of thunder above us.

To be honest I'd had enough of fighting witches now. I barely had the strength to stand up, let alone fight off another would-be soul-stealing crone. I peered into the fog, hoping the lifeboats had made it . . . and then I spotted a dark shape under the water again. For a millisecond I started to worry that it might be a kelpie, come to finish us off. But it wasn't – it was Brimstone, still a whale, and I noticed his tail was guiding something towards our rock. A broken piece of ship's timber. And sitting on it was something familiar. A small, green, terrified-looking chameleon.

'Brimstone!' I gasped. Young Brimstone. The old chameleon had rescued his younger self!

'Goodbye,' whispered the whale. 'Thank you . . .' Then he vanished.

Moments later I heard a splash and saw a black figure fighting its way through the sea towards us, sort of swimming, but not very well . . .

'Brimstone!' young Pallidia was shouting in a very un-witchy voice. 'Is it really you?'

Though of course young Brimstone couldn't talk so he just sat there, clinging to his wood, boggling us all like we were bonkers.

The sea was calm now, the fog was clearing, and as Pallidia reached us, the moon crept out from the last cloud and the air felt warm again.

'Brimstone!' Pallidia spluttered, hauling herself out of the sea and dancing towards him across the rocks like a ballerina. She scooped him up in her spindly arms. 'How did you get him back?' she demanded. And I noticed for the first time how blue and clear her eyes were. They were actually nice eyes – friendly eyes . . .

'The sea captain returned him to us,' I whispered, deciding a fib was definitely better than the truth.

'Really?' Pallidia smiled then. Not a witchy smile, but a happy teenager sort of a smile.

'He realised he'd made a terrible mistake. He felt bad and asked us to give him back to you.'

'Really?' Then she frowned at our clothes. 'You're soaking and your clothes are a mess. Come back with me and I'll give you some dry ones.'

But we didn't want to. We definitely didn't. Me and Ruby now realised how unstable a witch on the cusp can be, especially one as powerful as Pallidia. With a bit of luck she'd stay out of trouble for a few weeks, until the summer solstice of her sixteenth year (see I was picking up this witch stuff!) and then end up living on the bright side, sewing pants for a living. After all, as I told Ruby before, it would be better than stealing souls.

CHAPTER 21

We waited until Pallidia had found her rowing boat, thankfully unsunk and drifting nearby, then we waved her off. As she rowed back towards Middle Spit Sands, we shouted another fib – that our father, a fisherman, would be collecting us soon. Of course she didn't believe us. Who would? But I think witches prefer fibs to the truth sometimes.

'Wish I knew where Brimstone went,' said Ruby, as we squeezed the water out of the blanket. 'Old Brimstone, I mean.'

'Maybe he just ceased to exist once he'd found his young self,' I said, like a wise Jedi knight who understood everything about the mysteries of time travel.

'What?'

I tried to concentrate really hard. 'Well, while young Pallidia was cross, there was still a chance she'd turn bad and his destiny would be set – he'd become a talking chameleon – a familiar to a soul-taking witch. But once she'd got her pet back again and was happy then that future Brimstone ceased to be.'

'Really?'

I shrugged. To be honest I wasn't sure. Maybe he just preferred life as a witch-swallowing whale.

'Do you think this thing will ever fly again?' asked Ruby, as we clambered back on the blanket.

It didn't look promising. It was still full of water. The control panel was gummed up with seaweed and there were enormous scorch marks down the middle. Plus I reckoned the escaped mice had probably got into its engine, wherever the heck that was, because when we lay down on the thing and started it up I could hear squeaking from beneath us.

'If the timer works, when shall I set it for?'

Ruby shrugged. 'What about the day all this started, just before you climbed on to the blanket. What time was that?'

I tried hard to remember. 'I was eating doughnuts

when Bladderwart came into the shop, so it must have been near lunchtime.'

'Then set the time for a little bit before that.'

I pressed the time button. But nothing happened. I pressed it again. Still nothing. I smiled nervously at Ruby.

'Don't worry,' she said. 'You can always get a job at the circus – knife thrower's assistant, wasn't it . . . ?'

At the memory of the axes, I pressed the button extra hard and suddenly the blanket coughed into life like a half-broken lawn mower.

I was about to tell Ruby that I wasn't sure this was going to work, when suddenly everything turned blue . . . and the button with the clock and the calendar and the up and down arrows appeared. I set the numbers. 11:50, 02 06 12. Then I held my breath and waited and hoped.

'Tom! Tom? What do you think you're doing?'

I blinked a few times and rubbed my eyes, but the salt water was still making them sting.

'Tom? Wake up!'

'Dad?'

I glanced up bleary eyed. The salt was obviously messing with my mind too.

'Tom? Come on! Snap out of it, son.'

Then I realised it really *was* my dad, but I reached up and gave his nose a tug, just to be sure.

'Hey!' he said, brushing my hand away with a grin. 'What are you doing on the blanket?'

I sat bolt upright.

'And who's your friend?'

'What?'

Ruby was there next to me, still looking like she was asleep.

'And what the heck have you done with your hair?'

I touched my head and immediately got a shock of static from it.

Dad stared at me for a moment. A long, hard, knowledgeable stare. Then he smiled lopsidedly. It was a slightly worried smile, but happy at the same time. He shook his head and sighed. 'I'm glad you're home, son . . .'

And I knew then. He understood what had happened. Perhaps not *exactly* what had happened.

But something similar. I had danced on the dark side, but lived to tell the tale. Maybe that's how it had started with him too.

'Tom?' Ruby was sitting up now. 'We made it,' she rasped. Her voice as dry as mine. 'At least I think we did,' she added. 'Is this your shop?'

I nodded.

Dad meanwhile was on his hands and knees smoothing out the blanket. He fished out a stethoscope from his back pocket and held it against the blanket to listen.

'Mice,' he grimaced. 'In the cam shaft.'

'Yeah,' I said. 'It's needing a bit of work, to be honest – a full service and MOT, maybe . . .'

Dad grinned. 'Perhaps you could help me with that?'

'Sure,' I said. 'After all, that's what you pay me for.'

A little while later Ruby had gone to call her mum, and Dad had carted the blanket round the back to start the drying out process. As for me, I was sitting back at my desk with my feet up scoffing doughnuts when suddenly the bell above the door tinkled and a customer came in. I very nearly choked on a doughnut again. It was her – Bladderwart, the stench witch.

'Dad!' I squeaked. But there was no way he'd hear me – I was drowned out by the sound of a hair dryer, which he'd obviously started using on the blanket.

'Ruby!' I yelped. But she was still upstairs on the phone, explaining to her mum how she'd ended up in a town a hundred miles away from home when she was supposed to be at scout camp.

'Where's Jimmy?' Bladderwart growled.

I gulped. Her voice sounded like an old bloke's. An old bloke who smoked a pipe . . . *six* pipes (all at the same time).

I stuttered and stumbled, and tried to explain that he was out the back, when she held up a big hand to silence me. Then she opened her coat and produced a big black nylon bag.

'This needs mending,' she said, throwing it at me.

'We don't fix magical blankets that have a habit of going ballistic!' I said, throwing it back at her without a glance.

Her face crumbled into a frown. And her purple eyes flashed hotly. 'It's not a blanket. It's a lamp!'

'What?'

She tossed the bag back at me, and I realised that it was actually smaller and lighter than the blanket had been. And then I remembered that of course it couldn't have been the blanket stolen from bad Pallidia at a witchy meeting two weeks ago because bad Pallidia didn't exist (at least I hoped she didn't), she was now a happy and helpful old stitch witch, sewing pants somewhere . . .

'Tell Jimmy Gloria will be back at dawn,' rasped Bladderwart. 'And here . . .' she raked around in one of her coat pockets and produced a small purple purse. 'Half now, half later, just as Jimmy likes it'

I took the purse. And then watched her leave. For a second I considered not peeking inside the bag. After everything that had happened that would have been the sensible idea. But I couldn't help myself. I opened the bag and pulled out the lamp. It was like a cross between a lava lamp and one of those little metal lamps that Aladdin had . . . I watched it as the gloopy stuff inside glooped around hypnotically.

Then I remembered it wasn't actually plugged in, so it shouldn't be glooping at all. Then I did an extra silly thing. I gave the lid a rub . . .

Bang! There was a crash of yellow light. And suddenly something big and scary was looming above me with its arms folded, a seriously cross expression on his face.

'Oops,' I said, nervously.